BEAST

A Steele Riders MC Novel

C.M. STEELE

ISBN: 9798677628696

Copyrighted © 2020

All Rights Reserved

No part of this book may be reproduced, copied or transmitted in any form or by any means, electronic or mechanical, including photocopying, recording, or by any information storage or retrieval system without written expressed permission from the author, except in the case of brief quotations embodied in critical articles or reviews.

This is a work of fiction. Names, characters, businesses, places, events, and incidents are products of the author's imagination and are used fictitiously. Any resemblance to actual persons, living or dead, events or locales is purely coincidental.

Cover design: C.M. Steele

Cover Image: Deposit Photos

The use of actors, artists, movies, TV shows and song titles/lyrics throughout this book are done so for storytelling purposes and should in no way be seen as advertisement. Trademark names are used in an editorial fashion with no intention of infringement of the respective owner's trademark.

This book is licensed for your personal enjoyment. This book may not be re-sold or given away to other people. If you would like to share this book with another person, please purchase an additional copy for each recipient. If you are reading this book and did not purchase it, or if it was not purchased for your use only, then you should return it to the seller and please purchase your own copy.

Chapter One

Beast

After a long morning dealing with jury selection for a murder case, I finally arrive at the office. I have a couple of hours of work to do.

"Good afternoon, Mr. Brandon," Erica, the receptionist, greets me with a cheerful grin as I step off the elevator. She'd been hired a year ago to help manage most of the office tasks that aren't fulfilled by our paralegals.

"Good morning, Ms. Forrester. Is Francisco in?" My paralegal does his job well, and it's the only reason that he still has this job. He annoys the fuck out of me on a daily basis with his squirrely and nervous movements. He should be down the hall, doing research in our personal library.

"Yes, sir."

"Thank you. Please make sure I'm not disturbed for the next hour."

"Yes, Mr. Brandon."

When I enter my spacious office, I see the files and reference books with tabs marking the pages that I've requested have been added to my desk. There are three attorneys in this office, so the caseloads get sorted by seniority and priority. I'm a district attorney for Ellis County, which covers Steeleville and several other cities and towns. Most of the time I have a small caseload, but lately, with more cartel violence and hardcore drug busts, my load has increased. As soon as I prosecute and file away a case, another is slapped onto my desk. We weren't anywhere near as busy as Dallas County, but we had a much smaller team to handle the growing cases.

After scanning the complaints listed for each case, I run my hands through my short, freshly cut hair, hoping to get these cases to trial or settled soon. A knock at my door only increases my frustration because my ass wants to go home, but I know whoever is here to interrupt me will drag my day on. I check my watch, ready to ream Erica a new one, but it's been over an hour.

"Enter," I command, knowing it's my squirrely little assistant who is scared of his own shadow. Why he was given to me is confusing as fuck. I don't waste time, and having served in the Special Forces, I didn't have time for those who dilly-dallied when it was important.

"What do you need, Francisco?" I questioned, looking up at the sensitive young man. He stands there, rocking from one foot to the other.

"Um. Detective Spencer from Dallas is here to see you." We're not supposed to be meeting yet. He's lending a hand with information on the Cortes Cartel. I wonder if he has another lead for me.

"Send him in." Now he's someone I'd gladly kill time with.

"Hello, Charles," I stand, walk around my desk, and shake his hand.

"Hello, Will." He pulls me in for a one-armed hug. We've known each other for the past two years after teaming up on a major sex trafficking case. He's been an ally when it comes to the cartels.

Francisco lingers, knowing that I like to offer my guests a drink. "Take a seat. Would you like some coffee?" I take my seat.

"Sure, cream and sugar, please." I nod to my assistant, making sure he heard Spencer's preference.

"Same for you, sir?" my assistant asks, stammering in his words.

"Yes. Thank you, Francisco." He leaves, closing the door behind him. I'm glad to see him go. Why the hell is he so skittish around me?

"Damn, you have him shaking in his boots." He shakes his head and chuckles.

"I didn't do shit to him. It irks me that he seems afraid." I tap my pen on my desk and sigh. "Anyways, what brings you to see me? Anything I need to inform Steele about?" He knows that Boomer does what he has to do to keep his town safe and secure, even if it's skirting the law.

"No, um…" He doesn't seem nervous, but whatever brought him here, it's important.

Wrinkling my brow, I lean in with my elbows on my desk, and ask, "What's up, Charles?"

Looking to make sure the door is closed, he says, "I need to call in that favor already." Wow, that's quick.

"Yeah?" I question, wondering how big the favor is. He gave me some basic information that wasn't anything I couldn't get without a lot of leg work, but the fact that he showed up instead of calling tells me he needs something much bigger.

He opens his suit jacket and makes himself more comfortable, then continues, "I have a witness I need to put into protective custody, but she's as stubborn as a mule. She doesn't want to be alone where she knows no one."

"And you want me to do what?" I have a feeling where this is going.

"I want you to find her a lowkey job and place to stay in Steeleville. The population is small, and they won't know to look for her there."

"Is it just her?" Relocating when a witness has a family can be very difficult.

"Yes, she doesn't have any family and very few friends. She's a college student who works part-time as a librarian." If she doesn't have anyone, what difference does being alone make here or in fucking New York? Some people are very peculiar.

"We don't have a library in Steeleville," I inform him. The town is on the way up, but time and money play a big part in building new businesses.

"Damn, my ex-wife would say that's a travesty."

Chuckling, I nod. "I agree, but there are so many

other businesses that need to be built that actually make money." There's a light rap on the door, then Francisco walks in with a rolling cart and our coffees.

"Thank you. Can you prepare the Wilkins file for this week?"

"I'll have it done before I leave today."

"Fantastic." He leaves the office, closing the door behind him.

"Anyways, I want to take her away from that. You know if they are going to go hunting for her, they're going to check local libraries."

"So what led her to need WP?"

"She witnessed a shooting after locking up the library. She was almost to her car when Serrano noticed her. The next day, he'd been waiting for her. She turned around and went straight to the police. It was the best option for her." She's got brains. It's a no-win situation because of guys like that. That accidental encounter sealed her fate. She had to run.

He's got a very valid point. "How old is she?"

"Twenty." Damn, she's very young, but an idea strikes me. It's one place they might not try looking for her at.

"Then I know that she's not allowed to drink, but she can work at Panhandles. They're looking for a bartender. It's out of her element. There's a bakery being built, but it's not close to being ready. One of the Riders owns the bar, so we won't have any trouble."

"It might work. I think we can set that up. I need to move her today, so can you talk to your guys like right now?"

"I'll give Boss a call. He'll be discreet. But as to the matter of the apartment, I don't know if there's a place for her to stay."

His face falls as he grunts out, "Damn."

"You know, I have a spare bedroom in my house that I leave for one of the Riders should they need it. She can stay with me." I don't know why I offered; I'm not the type of person who gets along with strangers. Hell, even with the Riders, I'm still reserved. They know I'd help them out if necessary, but I don't like people in my home. As a lawyer, I have cases I can't discuss and having someone come in and start snooping around my place could damage my career and reputation.

He has a shit-eating grin on his face, giving him a much older look. "That can work. You're a damn saint. I can't thank you enough. The case should be coming up in January. After that, she can go back to her normal life, or so we hope." That's only three months away.

"What's her name?"

He lowers his voice to reply. "Mary Stark. She's agreed to change it to Mary Baldwin. Please give them a call over there and not a peep about it to anyone outside those you trust." Sometimes it's good to keep their first names, sometimes it's not, but since she's coming to Steeleville, I'm not worried about them finding her. The Riders are very protective of the town, and with surveillance systems in place, she would be more protected than anywhere else.

"Will do." Spencer knows that I can be trusted because I have no skin in the game. I don't owe anyone anything; that can't be said by many these days. So many people are under the thumb of the drug and human traffickers that you can't be sure who's still clean.

I walk him out to the elevators, waiting for him to get on before I head back to my office to give Boss a call.

Using a secure line, I dial Boss's secure line. We can't have anyone listening in for this girl's sake. "Hey, I need you to do me a favor. I'm sending in someone to take the job as a bartender. I can't say more than that, but she has no experience."

"Oh, okay. Work stuff?" he asks, knowing if it's a "need to know" situation.

"Yes. She'll be there in a little bit. I'm going to have her move into my guest bedroom that's set up at the house." I can't shake the feeling that this favor may be a dangerous one. I know nothing about the woman, and I can't really look her up because someone might be watching any record requests on her name.

"Hmm…really? Is there more I should know?" he asks, knowing my hatred for company.

"No, nothing like that. It's happening right away, so no time for anything else."

"Do you want me to take her to your place and get her settled?" They know the key code to my house because Cyber hooked up our houses with added or special security features.

"I won't be out of the office until eight, so that might be a good idea." It's Friday, and I refuse to work weekends, so I work late.

"Okay. After I show her around behind the bar and stockroom, I'll take her there."

"Thanks. I owe you one."

"I'll put it on your tab," he jokes. I hang up and get back to my files. Honestly, there's not that much, but I just feel that Steeleville needs me more. I'm tempted to toss in the towel and leave the D.A.s office to venture into private practice. I handle contracts for Boomer when he needs them, but mostly I'm good at destroying the defense and winning my cases.

I might leave work earlier because a part of me is already dreading having some random woman I never met staying in my home. God knows what she's going to be doing with my things.

I've got a damn headache building behind my eye. I'm extremely neat, and anything out of place bothers me a little, but when it's in my house, I expect it to be clean and organized all the time. The guys know that, so I tend to join them out or at someone's place, so they don't mess up my furniture or spill beer everywhere.

My desk phone rings, and it's the reception desk. "What's up?"

"Sir, I'm leaving for the night in about ten minutes. Do you need me to do anything before I go?"

"No. Thank you. Have a great weekend."

"You, too." She ends the call, and I check the time. Shit, the night has passed by in a blink of an eye. It's ten to five.

Chapter Two

Mary

I pack my things as quick as I can before they come looking for me. Last night the library was broken into, and the employee files in the office had been ransacked. Spencer called me this morning telling me to pack whatever I can and be ready to run. This perpetual fear of looking over my shoulder is freaking me out. I've already dropped ten pounds this week. Why the fuck did I have to witness a shooting? Fuck, I'm lucky I got away before the guy shot me too, but it now feels like a foregone conclusion that he'll get me.

A knock at my door sends the brush in my hands flying through the air. "Shit," I whisper. They probably heard that. Ducking down, I look through the bottom edge of the window and breathe a sigh of relief. It's just Detective Spencer.

I open the door and say, "You scared the shit out of me."

He quickly enters and closes the door. "Sorry, I didn't want to call you and have it traced. Are you ready to go?"

"You've found me a place?" I practically squeal.

"Yes, it's about an hour away in a remote town. It's safe, and you'll have a place to stay and a temporary job until this all blows over." I hug him, forgetting myself. He freezes and stiffens, so I pull away.

"Where?" I question, rocking back and forth on my heels. My inner child comes out. It's like when a kid is told they are going on vacation or that their parents have a surprise for them. Not that I got those moments in my life.

"I'll tell you on the way. I don't want to stay here any longer. It's not safe." I pick up my hairbrush off the floor, stuffing it in my bag, and then walk into my bedroom where my other bags are ready. "Is this everything?"

"Everything important." I leave my purse with my IDs and cards. I've already cleared out my bank accounts because I can't use it anywhere they can track me. It's scary and exciting, but mostly scary. He walks up and takes the heavier suitcase while I carry the duffle and my bookbag. Leaving my textbooks here makes me cry. They cost me a fortune in student loans that I can't get back, but maybe when it's all over, I can return to my old life.

We sneak into his car and pull away as inconspicuously as possible. It's insane how an everyday action changed my world from peacefully organized to living life on the run. I can't believe that I have to give up my life. Two and a half years of college for nothing.

"So, where are you taking me?" I ask him as he hits the dirt road a block from my apartment building.

"We're going down southwest to Steeleville," he states, checking his mirrors for anyone following us.

I play around with the name of the town in my head, but I can't place it. "I've never heard of it."

"Most people haven't. It's a small town that's just building up. You'll be safe there." A big knot develops in my stomach.

"We might be followed," I blurt out, panicking.

"Do you see anyone behind us?" He rolls his eyes at me like I'm acting too paranoid, but he doesn't have a killer hunting him down.

"The nearest car is about half a mile behind," I say, leaning back in my seat to get myself under control.

"It's going to be okay," he says, patting my hand. I nod, and then we settle into a silence. Although my mind hasn't stopped spinning through all the possibilities of what's to come.

After a few minutes, I'm back at my questions. "What am I supposed to be working as?"

"A bartender."

Immediately I'm freaking out. "What? I don't know how to do that! What if they come in there?" They couldn't be more off base than a bartender. I've got zero skills making drinks, and I'm not a people person.

"Calm down."

"Have you ever met a woman who 'calm down' actually worked on?" I'd punch him if he wasn't driving.

"Nope, but I'd hoped it would work on you. Anyway, the town is guarded by a group of bikers. Their President owns the town. He and his brother built it. They are good people. You'll be safe. They don't know your predicament. Only my friend Will is aware of the reason you need to hide, but he doesn't go by will in Steeleville. They call him Beast."

I slap my hands on my thighs. "Beast? You're expecting me to trust someone named Beast?"

"For someone in your predicament, you're very picky. Yes. I think he gets that name from his size and his skills as a lawyer because he's not even remotely like a beast. In fact, he's quiet and *calm* when he's not in a courtroom." He emphasized the calm like a dick.

Rolling my eyes, I bite out through gritted teeth, "Wow, a lawyer named Beast. Interesting. Is there a welder there named Beauty?"

"Ha-ha. Be nice. These people are going to be looking after you. Once you're protected by one, you're protected by all. The man you are going to be working for at the bar is called Boss. I'm not sure his real name, but he served with some of them in the military." Military men? Interesting.

"Really, okay. Well, it's better than being hunted by drug dealers and their associates," I sigh. Sliding down in my seat with my thoughts to myself, I'm finally resigned to my fate.

We reach the outskirts of Steeleville, and I swear I see a camera mounted on one of the utility poles. It's an odd place for a police camera. Maybe it's just a weather instrument. We do live in the wild west of weather.

Speaking of weather, I'm glad I'm inside an air-conditioned vehicle because it's a freaking scorcher.

Entering the town, I get the small-town feel. The main street is just like any other in the good old USA. Small shop buildings line the street although most of them seem vacant. Spencer mentioned that the town is new, so many of the businesses aren't operational yet. We pass the bakery he mentioned, followed by a tattoo shop where he pulls into a small parking lot next door. That's when I see the sign for a bar called Panhandles. "We're here."

"Yeah, can't miss it." I salute him. "Lead the way."

"Calm down," he barks out.

"Asshole," I mutter under my breath, but he hears me and laughs, opening the door for me. We leave my things in his car while we step inside. It's almost empty, but at this time of day, that's a very good thing because I'm already a bundle of nerves. A large man with salt and pepper hair and matching beard looks at us and smiles. "Welcome to Panhandles. Come sit." He taps the bar top, and we move to the stools in front of him.

"So what can I get you?" he asks, flipping a bar towel over his shoulder.

"I'm here for a job," I say, taking a seat on the stool with my elbows on the counter. I'm trying to remain cool, but this is all new to me.

"Name, sweet girl?"

"Mary Sta…Baldwin." Shit, I almost blew my cover. He knows it, but thankfully, he politely ignores my slip.

I'm Boss." He sticks a hand out over the bar top and takes mine. "It's a pleasure to meet you. You're here sooner than I expected." He looks toward the clock by the door. "So, where are your things?"

"I'll be back with them." Detective Spencer gets up and walks out.

Boss comes around the bar and says, "So, since you're going to be working here, I'm going to give you a quick tour of my pride and joy. You're training will actually start tomorrow. I don't have time for it today because I'm supposed to drop you off at Beast's place." He starts to lead to the back room, but I freeze.

"Beast's place?" I blanche because I'm going to be forced to stay in a place I don't know anyone and with a biker named Beast.

His brows screw up in surprise. "Yes. DA Brandon's home. I thought you knew that."

"No, I must have forgotten to ask. All I was told was that they found me somewhere to live and work."

He pats my shoulder and leads me to the storeroom with all the beer and bottles of liquor. "Don't worry, you don't have to fear Beast. Just stay out of his way and out of his things, and you'll be fine. He's grumpy when anyone invades his personal space."

I step back out into the corridor that leads back to the main bar area. "Ooh."

"Relax. I didn't mean to freak you out," Boss says, walking to the bar. "Come here and let me show you the set up behind here. We have two speedwells and two registers. Most nights, we only have two employees working. It's pretty safe here, but I still request that they are escorted out. One of the Riders will do it if I only have one person closing."

"Is everyone working tonight?"

"Yes, Fridays and Saturdays like all bars are our busiest nights. Roxie and Hans will work both nights. We're closed on Sundays."

"Kind of like Chick-fil-A?"

"Yes. So these are the beer coolers. Have you ever opened a beer before?"

"No, I haven't. Aren't some twist off, and some you need to pop off."

He puts two bottles on the bar and hands me a bottle opener. "Yes. Here's both. Open one of each for me. You'll learn which are which as you go. They can all be popped off it that makes it easier." I've seen this done before, so I do it like I'm a professional and it works. I'm jumping up and down like crazy, forgetting that I have a beer in my hands. It starts fizzing over.

The door opens and in walks a larger man with a thick beard, but he's in a dress shirt and a pair of jeans. He runs up to me, takes the beer, downing it in one long drink.

"Never waste a good beer." He winks and sets the empty bottle down on the top. I wonder if he's the Beast they mentioned. He's a handsome man, but then I spot a ring on his finger and know that if there's a wife at home, there's no way they wouldn't have told me that.

"Boomer. It's good to see you," Boss says with surprise, unnerving me a bit. Boomer?

"Hey, old man. Don't be hitting on the young girls in town. You're old enough to be her grandfather."

"He wasn't…" I exclaim, shaking my hands, trying to dispel his impression.

"Relax. I'm just jerking around."

"Boomer, let me introduce you to my new bartender, Mary. Mary, this is the mayor, president, owner, and well damn boss man of this town, Garrett Steele."

No one told me anything like that, but it makes sense at least. "Steeleville…ah."

"Nice to meet you. I'm sure you'll like it here. If any customer gives you shit, you let me or Boss know, understood?" Damn, okay. I feel like I'm talking to a mob boss and not the mayor of the town. I suppose when you're in charge of everything, you don't take shit from anyone.

"Yes, sir."

"Boomer is fine." He turns attention to Boss and says, "Now, can I have a word with you for a minute?" He tips his head to the back.

Boss nods. "Sure. Mary, why don't you walk around the bar and get acquainted with the setup. Next time don't shake a beer. I'll be right back." He winks and then follows Boomer to the back office. I practice moving around the bar when Detective Spencer enters with my things.

"Sorry it took so long. I had to take a call. Where did he go?"

"He went to talk to Boomer?" I point toward the back.

"Boomer, strange name for his position, but he bought the town after serving in the Special Forces and owning a demolition company."

"Oh, really. That explains a lot." Instantly, his name clears it up for me. I'm curious why they call Boss, Boss when it's really Boomer that's in charge. I don't want to ask because that would be rude, but I'm sure I will eventually.

"Don't be intimidated. They aren't the type to treat women badly."

"Thanks."

"I'm going to leave you now. If you need anything, you talk to Beast, and he'll get in touch with me. Here's a small stipend that should help, but I doubt they would let you pay for anything. Take care. I promise I'll do my best to get this resolved as soon as possible."

"Thank you for everything." He leaves just before the guys come from the back.

"Mary. Boomer's going to do me a favor and take you to Beast's house." I quirk my brow up and stiffen my shoulders, hating the change in plans even though this guy is supposedly so important. Those are the ones who have too much power and usually head into criminal activities.

"Mary, please. I don't know what's going on with you or Beast, but I promise you're the safest with any of the Steele Riders. If you want to call my wife, she'll tell you."

"No. It's just…" I stammer, looking for another excuse for my reaction.

"You don't need to explain, but I have to go pick up my wife from school. If you want, I'll take you to meet her, and then we can all head to Beast's place."

"Okay."

"These yours?" he asks, looking down to where Detective Spencer left my things.

"Yes." He picks them up easily, tips his head toward the door, and says, "Follow me."

"I'll see you tomorrow at ten AM, okay?" Boss says.

"Yes, thanks." I dip my head and blush, following Boomer to his large SUV. He opens the back passenger door and helps me in without letting go of my suitcase and duffle. I'm short as hell, so getting in his giant vehicle is difficult.

"Sorry, my wife rides in front with me."

"No. Not a problem. I understand." He closes the door and loads my things in the back before getting into the driver's seat.

"The drive isn't too far from here," he adds.

"So Boss says you're here temporarily, but if you need anything, we're always around."

About ten minutes later, we arrive at a small school, and he says, "Stay here," and then he steps out of the vehicle. He leans on the hood and makes a call. As soon as he hangs up, he moves to the front of the building. Another large muscular guy is standing by the door, and they shake hands. He has on a motorcycle vest thing that I've only seen on television. I can't read what it says, but I'm assuming it's one of the Steele Riders he mentioned.

A minute later, the guy leaves to another black SUV, and the front door opens to a beautiful, pregnant woman. Boomer takes her hand and her bag before leading her to the front passenger side.

"Hey, Crystal. I'd like to introduce you to Boss's new bartender. We're dropping her off at Beast's place."

"Beast's place?" Her brow arches and she eyes me with a bit of curiosity.

"It's not my business, and Beast asked us to leave it that way." He buckles her in, moving the straps to protect her and the baby without doing any damage and then gives her a tender kiss before closing the door. I swoon mentally.

"Hi, I'm Crystal Steele, Garrett's wife. Although I'm sure you already know that." The look on her face is a warning, and I read it loud and clear.

"Yes, and congrats on the baby." I don't have any interest in the man, but I'm sure she's still marking her territory. I like her.

"Thank you."

"Does Beast usually have work matters that you all handle that you're used to the secrecy?"

"No, but as a lawyer, we never hear about his cases. The man is as tight-lipped as they come. We all know that if you have a reason for silence then that's what it is. We're like a large family."

"Oh. I'm going to be bored at the house when I'm not working, it seems. I wish I had some books then."

"Well, girl, I've got those in spades, and I have an extra Kindle if you need it. The nearest bookstore is in Dallas, so this is the best we can do. Beast has a book collection, but he's very sensitive about people touching his things. Like very annoyed if anyone touches any of them.

"So everyone says."

"Well, let's get this show on the road," Boomer says as he jumps in the front seat.

We drove in companionable silence until Boomer asks his wife about her day. I watch them and wonder what it would have been like to have a family. I grew up in foster care, bouncing from place to place. It seems now as an adult, I'm doing the same thing.

We pull up to a small house with a large security gate. Boomer reaches out and enters a code on the pad along with his thumbprint. "New installation. Only a few of us have access. Sorry, but you'll be trapped here until Beast comes home. I promise you're safe here."

"Um…thanks." From looking at the setup, I'm guessing I most certainly am.

"Let us walk you in and show you the guest bedroom."

"He only has three bedrooms, but one is his home office." Boomer says and then jumps out, so I follow suit and nearly fall on my ass. He asks as he reaches Crystal's door. "Shit. Are you okay?"

"Just mortified but cool."

He helps his wife down, treating her like she's fragile. It's so freaking cute that I'm envious: to have someone that dedicated to your well-being and to love you so profusely.

He leads us inside to a very neat and clean home. It's so bare that it reminds me of a doctor's office or something, but it's not clinical. Modern, sleek but sterile.

"Down this way is the guest bedroom." I follow Crystal for the grand tour while Boomer grabs my things and brings them inside. It's a decent size with a full bed at the center and everything perfectly crisp.

"Beast's room is right down there." She points to the door opposite of mine and then she says, "The other side of the house is where the office and the kitchen are."

I throw up my hands in a mock-surrender. "Okay. Thanks. I'll stay out of his rooms."

"Well, we need to be going, but if you need anything, give me a call," she offers, slipping her arm around Boomer.

"Um…I don't actually have a phone." It's another thing I had to leave behind.

"No problem. I'm sure we can have that taken care of," Boomer answers.

"Oh, no. Please don't. I'll be fine." They nod, but something in their posture lets me know that they are just humoring me. Crystal reaches out and gives me a hug.

They leave, and I'm all alone in this immaculate house, letting the loneliness seep through my bones. Sitting on the bed, I wonder what the hell I'm supposed to do until he comes home.

A rumble in my stomach reminds me that I pretty much haven't eaten today. Please tell me there's more than some crackers. It only takes a minute for me to find the kitchen. If the house is neat, the kitchen is pristine. It looks like it came straight out of an expensive magazine or someone's dream kitchen on Pinterest and hasn't been used yet. I run my hand over the black, white and grey granite countertops, trying not to drool. A part of me is glad that I'm here by myself, so I don't look like a nut.

I start to dig in the cabinets and then into the fridge, deciding what I can make. I find everything for spaghetti, I quick thaw some Italian sausage and then get to cooking a quick sauce, chopping the veggies like this was my own kitchen. I'm in the middle of dumping the veggies into the pan with the sautéed sausage when the grease pops, shocking me, and I jump back, hitting the spoon that I used to stir the sauce, sending a splatter of bright red everywhere including his beautiful white cabinets and my face.

I run to the guest bathroom and grab the towels hanging nicely. Shit, I cringe using them, but some bleach should get them back to the pristine white.

I do my best to clean the kitchen and then turn everything off. I have to wash up. There's no way I can meet him looking like a disaster after dirtying his kitchen. I get to my temporary room and go into the bathroom to shower. I'm naked by the time I realize that there aren't any towels in there. Shit. I hope there are towels in the other bathroom. I leave the room, believing I'm alone, but I'm not.

Chapter Three

Beast

Regret strikes me, knowing that there's a complete stranger with a shit load of baggage invading my private space. I do my best to push through the rest of the day without freaking the fuck out. Staying late suddenly doesn't hold any merit. Now I want to get home and make sure she's not sneaking into rooms, snooping around my office.

As I make the thirty-minute drive back home, I call Boss. He's busy at the bar, and it's a little loud since it's the start of a long Friday night. He shouts over the crowd, "Sorry, Beast, can't talk. Be nice." I make my way to the house, hating that he couldn't tell me anything about her. Boomer sends me a text. *Took her to your house for Boss.*

I call him right away since I'm driving and can't respond. "Hey, don't freak out."

"I'm not. I'm just driving." I partially lie because I don't trust people. Maybe it's a lifetime of being a part of a secret operations team or the fact that I'm a lawyer. Either way, I never trust people or their motives, especially in my home. "She's set up in the guest bedroom. Crystal says we're going to need extra guys on her. She's hot—her words, not mine."

"Hot? That's all I need. I don't have time to babysit. She's not bringing people into my home no matter who tickles her fancy for the night. This is a bad idea. I should set her up somewhere else."

"She's safest there, but I'll see what I can do."

"Thanks." We hang up, and I feel a little bit of relief. I creep into my place, attempting to catch her by surprise to see if she's doing something manipulative. Shit. If she stays, I might have to get some cameras inside my house. I'm losing it. This woman hasn't done anything wrong. In fact, she's the witness to something terrible and is willing to testify despite the danger to her.

I enter the house and don't hear anything. I set my keys and briefcase down in the front hall and then remove my suit jacket. I head toward my bedroom and start to drag my tie off when I freeze. Holy motherfucking hell. My houseguest is standing buck naked in the hallway between our rooms.

Naked.

Brain, work. Damn it, function.

It's short-circuited when all the blood pooled in my ten-inch cock. She's short with killer curves: large, round breasts with dark pink nipples pebbled probably from the cool air. I can't even hide the reaction in me. My cock comes to life like it's never done before. I swallow hard, wondering why I've been tortured with this sweet felony like an untouchable, forbidden fruit.

"Where the fuck are your clothes?" I growl out, thinking…what if Boomer or Boss came to check on her and saw her like that…

Naked.

Bared.

Mine.

An insane rush of jealousy turns me into a bigger prick than I can be. Spencer should have warned me that she's a fucking goddess.

Long black hair, bright blue eyes, and puffy pink lips that are parted so temptingly make her face unmistakably perfect. My dick is more than alive, he's unbearably hard as I picture her on her knees with those pouty lips wrapped around my cock, pleasing me and thanking me for letting her stay.

"Shit." She dashes back into the guest room like a frightened kitten. She should be because I'm feeling dangerous.

I don't know if it's my anger at the situation or my desire for her that has me worked up. Hell, I want to pick her up by her pert, round ass that bounces so deliciously, carry her off to my bed, and then nail her to the mattress until she comes with my name on her lips. I storm toward the door, knocking hard. Hell, I could have used my dick; it's so damn stiff.

I attempt to take a calming breath to rein in the overwhelming rush of lust. "Mary."

"I'm sorry. Oh God," she sighs, pressing her naked

form against the door. I can hear the shift on the wooden frame, doing nothing to slow down the desire.

"I'm not God." Although, I feel like I need to repent for my sins all of a sudden. Maybe if I'm good, I'll be blessed with her sexy curves to explore. Right now, she's a temptation I can't have. I'm officially in hell.

"Sorry. I was about to get in the shower, and there were no towels. I wanted to hurry so you wouldn't know, but oh hell. This is terrible." There should have been towels in there. At the very least, I had towels hanging on the towel racks. The rest should be in my room or in the laundry.

"I'm sorry. I'll grab some and leave them outside the door." I rush off to my room and grab the only towel I have left. Shit, I have to do some laundry. It's something I do every weekend. I knock on the door. "Sorry, this is the only one left. I'm supposed to do laundry tomorrow."

"Thank you," she whispers, embarrassment clear in her voice. The gut-wrenching feelings of frustration and pleasure hit me because if I'd been up on my laundry or bought more towels, she wouldn't have had this moment of mortification. I walk away to give her privacy, but the first thing I do is head into the laundry room and start a load of towels.

Once I come back out, the smell of food hits my nose. I'd been so damn preoccupied with my sexy guest that I didn't notice the food. I walk into the room and see that she was in the middle of cooking before I got home. Two towels are in the sink soaking. Ah, and that's where my missing towels went. She had a mishap.

"Fuck, it smells fantastic." My dick twitches as I bring the spoon to my lips. Seriously, it's delicious. The thought of stopping her in the shower and licking off any sauce she managed to get on herself hits me, and I let out a low groan. Grabbing my cock through my dress slacks, I give it a squeeze to warn my shaft to chill out.

Getting ahold of myself, I roll up my sleeves and help with the food. I turn the stove back on and grab a pot of water to start the noodles. I wash the used dishes while I wait for the water to boil. Just as I turn off the water, she comes into the kitchen with a gasp.

"Is everything okay?" I ask her, realizing that she had been staring at my ass and now has her eyes trained to my hard fucking cock.

Her head immediately jerks up. "Oh yeah. Don't mind me. It's just…I'm sorry. I was going to clean up my mess," she stumbles on her words, looking adorable in a pair of light grey joggers and a cute tank top. She's wearing a thin bra that's not helping hide those ridiculously stiff nipples that I want in my mouth.

"It's fine. I was just trying to help. I'm hungry."

"Thank you. For everything. I didn't mean to totally flash you. It seems I have really bad timing."

"It would seem that you're not lucky in that area, yes?" I am, though.

She wobbles just a bit, planting her hand on the counter. Staring at where her hand lands, I can see it's shaking.

"Are you okay?"

"Yeah, I just didn't eat today."

"Wow. You should have grabbed a snack." I'm

pissed that she's not taking care of herself. It's okay because I'm here to do it now.

"I'm already freeloading off your generosity. I didn't want to eat all your chips." I shrug. I have tons of bags of chips. It's one of my few vices. I love to have some beer with some chips after a long day at work.

"Sweet felony, you're welcome to it all."

I open the cabinet and pull out a bag of Lays and hand it to her. She snatches it and takes one like she's starving. I knew it. "Sweet felony?"

"Yes. Nothing like having a witness under my protection with a body that's fucking criminal." She blushes, and I know I've crossed the line. "Forgive me. It's just well…it's best that it was only me coming home."

"Why? Do you have a girlfriend or something?" Yes, her, but it's too fucking soon. I have to wait until the trial to make a move. It's unethical and an abuse of power even though I'm not on the case.

"No, but if Boss or Boomer came to check on you, that would have ended badly." I have to rein in this jealousy. She's not mine even if I wanted. She's under my protective custody.

"Why? Well, I get why Boomer seeing me would be bad because Crystal would bury me."

"Wait, you met her?" I could see Crystal being fiery with her if she looked at Boomer wrong.

"Yes, he wanted to pick her up before he brought me here. She's really nice and really pregnant." And you will be too, one day very soon. I never considered having babies until this very second, but that's what I want as

Beast

long as she's the woman I put them in. My dick stiffens, and I close the gap between us.

"Let me finish dinner. Sit down." I do my best to control the need to kiss her, so I pull out the chair and wait for her to take it.

"You don't have to be so nice to me just because I showed you all my goodies." She playfully teases to ease her own embarrassment.

"I know that, but I didn't get a great look, so although I saw most of your sexy silhouette, I didn't get a full image. I still feel bad about it either way."

"You shouldn't; it wasn't your fault."

"But the next time you give me a show, just know I might not just watch."

She gasps, flushing from her chest up to her neck with mortification. I should be embarrassed about how I'm acting. I've never been this forward with a woman before. I never said more than a sentence at a time. Now I can't stop letting her know how much trouble she's in by staying here.

My phone pings just at that moment. I pull it out and see a message from Boomer. ***I have a place for her to move in tomorrow.***

Immediately I'm stricken with the idea of her being around other men. Another bastard looking at her the way I am. Cock hard and ready to strike. I can't have her, but that doesn't mean I'm tossing her to the wolves.

Never mind. She's staying here.
Are you sure?

She's staying. I wonder if he can feel the growl in my words because even though I just typed them from the look on her face, Mary certainly heard me growl like the beast they call me.

Understood.

"Would you like something to drink?" I ask her, trying to maintain control of the beast inside of me. The nickname came from war and my size, but it has a new meaning now. I feel animalistic around this small little beauty.

"I can get it for myself." She moves to stand, but I give her a shake of my head.

"I'll get it. Sit," I bark out.

"Are you always so bossy?" She crosses her arms under her breasts with a humph, fucking driving me nuts.

I bent down in front of her, cupping her chin. "Yes." Unable to stop myself, I kiss her forehead. "Now, what would you like?"

"Um…do you have a soda?" I try to not focus on the fact that she liked that invasion of her personal space.

"Sure." I open the fridge and pull out two kinds. "I'll take the Sprite."

"Did you want garlic bread?"

"Um…sure." She takes a drink of her Sprite, and I watch, amazed and jealous at the damn can that touches her soft lips. "Do you like to cook?"

"Not really, but it's not like there's a lot of food options here."

"Your kitchen's gorgeous, though." She looks around in awe. Her pretty face pleased with it all. It makes me want to attack her lips and tell her it all belongs to her now.

Instead, I mutter, "Yeah, Morgan decorated it."

"Morgan? An ex." A thump in my chest loves the hint of jealousy in her voice. It's unmistakable, and she realizes it.

I shake my head and then slide the garlic bread in the oven. "No, Boomer's sister."

"Oh. She's an interior designer?" It's an innocent question, but I wonder if she's still insecure. There's no reason for her to be bothered by any woman in Steeleville.

"No, I just figured she was the only one around with shit to do, so I asked her."

"She doesn't work?"

"Well, she's starting to now. She's going to open a cafe in town and is married to another Steele Rider," I remark, straining the pot of noodles.

"Are you a Steele Rider?" I nod.

"Are you outlaws?"

I turn and crack a smile. "I'm a lawyer, sweetheart."

"So that's a yes." The playfulness is back and even more of a turn on. Shit. I'm a lost soul.

"You're a brat." A giggle escapes her lips, and she shrugs slightly before bringing that damn can to her lips.

"Thanks." She winks at me as she sets it down on the table, shamelessly flirting. I love it and hate it all at once. I go back to the stove and finish up the dinner without another word. I want to ask a million questions, but I can't and shouldn't be getting involved.

The timer goes off on the oven, and I pull out the perfectly toasted garlic bread. "Dinner is done."

"Wonderful." She stands to lend a hand with the

dishes. We're close enough that I used the closeness as an excuse to steal a simple touch. Her arm brushes against mine and my cock jerks in my pants like I'm a teenaged boy getting my first touch of a girl. Holy hell, I'm a fucking creep.

We sit down in companionable silence for a few minutes as I watch her slide the fork past her lips. "So I want you to know that regardless of what happens, you're safe here. I'm not going to let anyone get to you. Okay?"

"Yes." Disbelief crosses her face.

I lean forward and sincerely say, "I promise you're safe. I'd do anything to keep you safe."

"I don't think I'm safe from you," she confesses.

I sit back, taking in what she said because she's right and wrong. I don't plan to give in to the lust-filled passion clouding my brain, but if she says the word, I'll devour her. "You are. Until the day you tell me that you want me to strip you bare and lick you from head to toe."

"See. It's talk like that. It's…"

"It's what? Frightening you." Shit, I don't want to scare her away.

She looks up at me, biting at the edge of her bottom lip, and then whispers, "No. It's tempting."

"You're a walking felony, Mary."

"I'm actually legal."

"I know." I let out a disappointed sigh and then set down my fork. "I'm done eating. Are you?"

"Yes." She stands, taking her plate and reaching for mine, but I get up as well, no longer ashamed of the fact that my cock refuses to go down. "Wow," she whispers.

"Yeah, well, you know where I stand, and so does he, so we can just pretend that it's not there." Her existence is my own aphrodisiac.

"It's kind of really hard to miss."

"Tell me about it." I set my plate in the sink and then adjust my bulge, so it's not ripping through my zipper.

"I'll wash the dishes," she offers. Mary has no idea what little will power I have at the moment. She's not opposed to the attraction between us. If she wasn't under my protective custody, she'd be under me right now, crying out my name.

"No, don't do them. I'll take care of it. Get some sleep. You've been through a lot today."

"Thank you," she says, stepping up on her tippy toes, placing a kiss on my cheek. It takes all of my strength to not turn and drag her in for a real kiss. She leaves the room, and I feel like I can breathe again.

I make quick work of the kitchen cleaning. It's one of the many things I learned at boarding school, and I've always made sure things were clean to avoid punishment, now it's just who I am, but at least I'm quick at it.

Once it's done, I turn off the light and remember the towels. I go in to change them only to find, Mary bent over, halfway inside the washer, digging out the towels. I let out a low growl. "I'm starting to think you're intentionally trying to destroy my control."

She pops up to dump the towels into the dryer. "Sorry. I just thought I'd help." She closes the dryer door and sets the machine. When she turns around to look at me, I see that I've upset her.

"Goodnight," she murmurs, but I can't let her leave thinking that I'm upset.

Hard as hell and hornier than I've ever been, but I'm not upset with her at all. I reach out and grab her wrist, dragging her to me. "I'm sorry I'm a dick."

I snake my hand around her jaw, my thumb rubbing across her chin.

"I've been messing up your world, so I get it." She softly attempts to pull away, but the fight really isn't in her. I hold her close, looking down into her soft, light eyes.

"You're making it hard, but it's insanely fucking better. Goodnight, beautiful." I brush my lips across hers, gently before letting her go and walking away to my room.

"Fuck," I muttered to myself, taking off my clothes and heading to bed. I need a cold shower, but I don't even have towels to dry off. Luckily I'm home for the day, but that doesn't help with the damn hard cock. Closing my eyes, I attempt to go to sleep, but it's only eight. Shit. I slip on some joggers and head into the living room to watch a movie. This is going to be a long night.

Chapter Four

Mary

I DON'T HAVE ANY IDEA HOW I MADE IT THROUGH THE night. I heard him leave his room shortly after I got in bed, but I never heard him come back. I wonder if he left the house or slept on the sofa, but I'd been too afraid to look. Damn it. I don't know how I'm going to get to work, and I'm afraid to even see him. The man is so gorgeous and sweet. He has to be over six three at the very least with broad shoulders to match. I nearly keeled over, seeing him with sleeves rolled up, cooking. Everything from his thick almost-black hair down to his sexy thighs made me melt.

I've found men attractive before. I even tried dating when I first got to college, but I couldn't let myself go all the way. It's not like I intentionally saved myself or anything, I just never found someone worthy, even temporarily, to give my virginity. Hell, so far every Steele Rider I've encountered was handsome. How that ratio is possible, I don't know, but then again, I've only met like four of them so far. Now, Beast, on the other hand, is sure as hell looking like hands down the winner, but that's just the lusty way he looks at me. "It's just pure lust," I remind myself.

A knock at the door startles me. "Mary, would you like some coffee?"

"Yes, please. I'll be there in one minute." God, I swear I don't know how I'm going to manage if he kisses me again. Better yet, how will I manage if he doesn't? Damn that kiss—panty-melting, soul claiming kiss. How could I forget something so perfect? This is all confusing. For the first time since the incident, I completely forgot about the threat to me.

Finally, I get myself under control and step out of the room. Beast isn't in the hallway which gives me a brief moment to steel my emotions. When I reach the living room, he's on the phone with someone so I move toward the kitchen to let him talk while I grab my coffee. Quickly, I turn to leave and steal a glance at his ass.

"No, I need you to get this trial over with. I'm not a fucking babysitter, Spencer." I gasp, doing my best to maintain my control because I want to cry. That's what he thinks of me. I understand, and now I'm going to do my best to keep my distance. I can't just go anywhere, but at least I can avoid him. Maybe I can get some books from Crystal like she offered. I walk into the kitchen and lean against the counter, trying to think of my next move.

He comes into the kitchen a little tenser than earlier. "I'm going to drop you off at Panhandles," he grumbles, moving past me to pull out two coffee mugs. I'd been so lost in his painful words that I forgot all about the coffee.

"You don't have to do that." Apparently, I'm already a burden to him, so I need to just get on with making the break.

"Actually, I have to do it because you don't have a car and it's not safe for you to go by yourself." He's more irritated by the second.

"Sorry, I can ask Boomer if there's a small apartment in town near the bar." It would be easier if I could stay somewhere closer to the bar and away from Beast.

"What part of you're not supposed to be alone, don't you get?" He practically snarls at me. I want to kick him in the nuts.

I slam my hands down at my sides, clenching my fists. Taking a deep breath, I put a teaspoon of sugar in my coffee and then finally gain enough control to say, "Damn it. This is stupid. I should just refuse to testify, so I can go back to my normal life."

Immediately he seems pissed off. "Not going to happen. They won't let you live even if you didn't tell, just in case one day you have a change of heart."

"You know that you're not going to take me every day you work." The look of utter dismay covers his handsome face, almost making me laugh.

"You won't be working a lot. This is a part-time job just to keep you busy. Boss has two employees who work most days." The snooty motherfucker is pissing me off. I can't work, I can't leave, and he doesn't want me here.

"I need money to survive, so I need to work."

"Anything you need will be picked up by me." He

steps closer to me, causing me to move backward until my ass hits the sink.

"Seriously, I'm not your responsibility," I say, puffing out my chest.

He tips his chin up at me with his brow arched. "Actually, you are."

"Well, hopefully, you'll get your wish and the trial will come sooner."

He starts laughing in my face, pissing me off. I glare at him which stops the humor in his expression. He grasps my chin firmly, but he's not hurting me. He leans in and says, "Oh, so this nonsense is about what you overheard. I get it. Well, listen, sweet felony. Although it's not illegal to fuck your brains out—it's unethical. I can't wait for the time to pass because the second the trial is over I'll be taking you hard and long. So what I told him was to get this moving along. Not because I don't want you, but because I want to stake you to my mattress with nothing but our sweat between us. Until then, I'm going to do my best to avoid temptation. Drink your coffee, and I'll work on some breakfast after I start another load."

He leaves the kitchen and heads towards his office and the laundry room. I finish making my coffee with my hands shaking. The man looks tired but still hot as hell. Something about the way his messed up hair and extra facial hair adds to his level of hotness. It's insane how attracted I am to him. He calls me a felony, but he's the one whose looks should be criminal. I bet he wins cases because the female jury members fall over themselves to please him. I take my cup, hoping to sneak back in my room to get dressed. I stop as I pass the living room to see at least three loads of laundry folded on the sofa, stacked neatly.

"Did you sleep at all last night?"

"A little, but I waited for the dryer to be done so I could fold them and start on the rest of my laundry."

"Oh, okay. Well, if there's anything you want me to do while I'm here, just let me know. I don't want you to go through all that trouble for me."

"Good. Your laundry's your own responsibility." I nod and walk off. Entering the bedroom, I pull out a nice pair of jeans with a tank top and hoodie. Sweeping my hair in my hands, I pull it up into a tight ponytail and then pin back a few stray hairs with some bobby pins. I packed all that I could take with me which thankfully included my makeup and hair stuff. I may have worked in a library; however that didn't mean I had to look plain and boring. Staring into the bathroom mirror, I take in my appearance. "I look cute," I say, winking at myself. Boss didn't say anything about what to wear, so I'm assuming I don't need to dress up. Just to make a good impression, I do put on my makeup like a pinup. I don't usually put on this much, but it's a bar and people tip better when you look sexy.

Chapter Five

Beast

I NEARLY DROP THE DAMN BACON ON THE FLOOR WHEN she steps into the kitchen. She's fucking perfect and too sexy to be working at the bar. It's going to take my entire being to get ahold of these emotions she's awoken in me. A devious look in her eyes tells me she wants me to notice or snap about how hot she looks, but as much as I'd love to make her change, I have to remember that I have no right—just yet.

"You look nice. Breakfast is going to be small since we only have about twenty minutes before we have to leave." I slide over a plate with some scrambled eggs and bacon. "Excuse me. I need to change."

The second I enter my bedroom, I close the door and lean on it to catch my breath. I've spent years in wars, stood across from the enemy in the desert sands and across the courtroom and yet I've never felt this afraid. Mary terrifies me, and I'm not sure why I can't fight this pull. She's sexy to be sure, but I'm not a thirty-five-year-old virgin. I've never dated a woman I didn't find attractive. Not that there's been that many women in my life to begin with and a lot less that I actually had sex with. Shit, maybe that's my problem I'm fantasizing over a barely legal woman because I haven't had sex in five years.

That's the excuse I'm going to tell myself because there's no way I can admit to more, or I'll never make it to the trial. I dress in a pair of jeans and a tight black t-shirt stretched over my chest and then pop on and lace up my black combat boots. Slipping on my leather vest, I plan to ride out as soon as she's at work. I need to clear my head, and nothing works more than riding on my Harley. When I step out into the hall, Mary lets out a gasp. "Wow, night and day." She licks her lips unconsciously.

"Yeah. Ready?" I pretend to not notice her reaction.

"Yes."

I lead her out to my reinforced SUV that Wrench upgraded for all the Riders after the attack on Crystal. It happened a couple of months back, and then we were attacked again, nearly killing Mick. The fucking Cartels are making our lives difficult around here, but as a DA, they are trying to avoid fucking with me. Still, we can't be too careful. I open the door and help her in. As soon as she's sitting, I close the door and run to the other side and hop in.

I don't say anything until we're about a block away from the bar. Most of the time I don't talk outside of work, having said more than enough for the whole day, but I want to speak to her. "Call me when you are done, and I'll come to pick you up."

"It's Saturday. Who knows how long I'll be there. Don't the bars stay open until like one in the morning? Can't I ask someone else to take me to your place?"

"No. Call me."

"I don't have a phone or your number." I forgot that she left in a rush and taking her phone was too risky.

"Yes, about that. I'll pick one up and drop it off at the bar with my number programmed in." She's huffing and puffing in her seat with her arms crossed, but I'm not in the mood to argue with her. The thought of someone else driving her home in the middle of the night is too damn much for me. Besides, she's not going to work no damn fifteen hours. Fuck, I don't want her to work at all, but again, I don't have a right to say shit.

We barely pull into a parking space at the bar when she jumps out. Fucking shit. I do the same after turning off the engine. I follow her inside the bar, and both Boss and Roxie are there. She works there several times a week. It makes me feel better that it's not Hans. He'll be closing tonight.

"Mary, Beast, welcome," Boss cheers. He makes introductions and then shoos me out. "We don't open for another two hours."

I start to walk back toward the door but stop to add. "I'll be back to drop off her phone."

"She gets out at four. I don't want to work her too much on her first day," Boss says. Thank fucking God I don't have to pull him aside to keep her from working late at night.

"Good." I walk out, itching to touch her, kiss her goodbye. Storming over to my ride, I get in, take a deep breath, and then pull out onto the main road. I want to go for a ride, but it's going to have to wait. First thing's first is the phone. I drive to Dallas for it because I don't want anyone to link her to Steeleville until this is all over. I pick up a non-contract phone that's untraceable to prevent any names being tracked. Plugging in my number before leaving the store parking lot, I drive off with a smile on my face.

When I get back into Steeleville the bar is open for the day. I parked out front because I wasn't staying no matter how much I wanted to sit at the edge of the bar and scowl at any fucker that tries to hit on her.

Entering Panhandles, I see five customers inside. It's still very early, but it's a Saturday when people tend to be off. I'm not familiar with them because I'm not the sociable type. Mary spots me and starts. I move toward her, loving the way her eyes are trained on mine.

"Here it is." I move to hand over the device, but I think better of it and keep it from her. First, I have to give her a warning. "Don't be giving guys your number. Not one motherfucking guy. Understood?"

"Yes, sir." She rolls her eyes, snatches it from my hand, and tucks the phone in her back pocket. "Thanks, Beast."

"No problem. I'll be here at four." I don't stay to talk, and I don't bother to look back because it's all I can do to keep my distance. The longer I watch her, the worse it's going to get.

As I leave the bar, I see her reflection in the lighted

Beast

beer sign. A deep rumble rips through my chest, sounding like the roar of my engine. Fuck, I need to get her out of my head before I act on the lust rushing through my body. The ride to my house feels eternal, even though it's a few minutes away.

The second I pull into the gate, I park my ride next to my Harley, get out and then jump on my bike. The wind hits my face, the cool air helps calm my cock down, but it's not enough to keep it down for long. Envisioning Mary working behind the bar as bastards steal glances at her breasts, stealing my smiles from her, pisses me off.

I drive around on my bike, and for the first time in my life, I find no relief in it. When I make it back to my house, I strip and jump in the shower, turning it full blast on cold. I'm frozen two minutes later and I manage to finally make the fucker surrender. Once I'm out and wrapped up in a towel, I picture Mary with a towel wrapped around her body, tucked in at her breasts to hold it in place because heaven forbid she accidentally offer me a free show again. The image is too much and I have the towel on the floor while I'm fisting my cock, stroking the fucker until I blast my nut all over my hand and onto the bathroom tiles. It's completely obscene the way I made a mess. It belongs buried deep inside her pussy and not on my floor. Grumbling, I clean it up and take another damn shower.

The rest of my Saturday is ruined by thinking about her working in a bar. How the fuck am I supposed to last until the trial?

The rest of the day, I pace the house, looking for

something to take my mind off her. Whipping out my briefcase, I work on my upcoming case to see if there's any way to tighten up the loose ends. Page after page, there's nothing to help me. The case is airtight. I'm not even sure why this guy doesn't plead guilty already. The sentence would be a lot lighter. The alarm on my phone goes off. I'm off my sofa and tucking the file back in my briefcase. Time to go get my future baby mama.

I'm up and out of the house, running down to my truck, and on the road within five minutes. I pull up to the bar and the lot's half full. When I get in, Mary's eyes jump straight to the door, and she blushes.

I tap my watch, and she shrugs, pouring another beer.

When I walk up to the bar, the guy she's serving sees me, takes the beer, and smartly, goes back to his table of friends. No one—and I mean no one—should even consider coming in between us. Even if at the moment there really isn't an us.

"Sorry. I'm done now." She puts the money into the register and sets the guy's change on his table before walking to the back to get her things.

Boss comes over to see me. "Hey, Beast. Everything okay?" We shake hands as he hands me a beer. I need this shit to calm my nerves.

"Yeah, why wouldn't everything be okay?" I ask, trying to play it off, which is pointless because anyone can see right through me when it comes to her.

"Because you look ready to murder a guy." He laughs, but I do not see the humor in this. I'm ready to kill a motherfucker for looking at my girl let alone speaking to her. I've no right or reason to be this crazy possessed over her, and it's driving me nuts. One whole day and this girl has me wrapped around her little finger.

"No, just setting some ground rules." I set down the empty bottle on the bar top.

"Ha, so that's how it goes?"

"I'm just doing my job," I lie.

"Ah, yes. I understand. Well, she's done until Monday. Same time," he adds as Mary comes up to us.

I nod, we shake hands again, and then I lead Mary out. "Thanks for picking me up. I didn't realize how tired working in a bar could make me." I'd carry her out of this place, but I don't want to look like a nut. As soon as we get into the truck, I buckle her in. I can see she's sleepy.

"Are you hungry?" I ask, driving back to the house as she relaxes against the seat.

"Yes, but I'd prefer a nap."

"Okay. I'll make something, and you can sleep."

"Oh, no. I can't do that to you. I'm not lazy, you know?" There she goes with her sexy feistiness even though she's sleepy. Damn, I find it sexy as fuck.

"I know." She finished her first day at a new job that I'm sure isn't easy. As a librarian, I'm sure she sat a lot, shushing the kids and stocking returned books. I'm not quite sure what else happens because I haven't been to a regular public library since I was a teen, but it's not the same as standing and serving drinks all day.

"Never mind. I'll help you cook and then have an early night."

"I will cook, and you will nap. End. Of. Story."

Sleep didn't come for me last night. I'm exhausted as I start the coffee this morning. Last night she slept like a baby after I fed her a small meal. As soon as the coffee's set and brewing, I head back to my room to shower and change. Pulling out my lounging clothes, I step into the shower and let the cold water seep into my bones. Looking after Mary only made my need for her double. My cock needs a reminder that she's off-limits.

Once I get out, I wrap a towel around my waist and then walk back into my bedroom and sit on the bed. Thinking for a minute turned into twenty. A knock at the door startles me. "Yes," I call out.

"I brought you a cup of coffee."

"Thanks. I'm coming now." I quickly stand up and dress and then open the door. She's standing there with her long hair in a ponytail and two coffee cups in her hands.

"Thanks, Mary. You didn't have to do that."

"It's nothing. Thank you for dinner last night. I don't think I even mentioned it before falling back to sleep."

"You're welcome. Are you feeling well-rested?"

"Yes, but you don't look like it."

"No. I couldn't sleep."

"Sorry. I know you don't like people in your space."

"It's not that. Are you hungry?"

"Actually, I started breakfast. You relax, and I'll cook this time."

"I'm not even going to argue about that."

"Good, now go sit down and chill or whatever you do." The sight of her walking into the kitchen is the last thing I remember as I fall asleep on my sofa.

Chapter Six

Beast

It's been a week since my world has been flipped on its head. My future wife loves her job even though she comes home exhausted. Even though I'm worn out, I've hardly slept a wink since she arrived. She's captivated me day and night. So far we've managed to keep our distance. The only time I see her is before and after work. Usually, our conversation is short and to the point.

After some delays, the trial of the suspected bank robber who shot one of the guards begins today. It's unusual to proceed with a trial on a Friday, but we're forced to do so because the calendar is packed. We're limited unless we want to move a trial to another jurisdiction, which isn't particularly good for the prosecution.

I'm in court for the next two weeks, making it difficult to take Mary back and forth to work. I informed Boss that she would be working on my schedule for the time being or not at all. I've already warned him that men need to stay away from her, but I'm not sure how good that's working.

By the time I'm done making my opening statement, the defendant leans over to his lawyer and whispers something. I don't hear it, but I have a feeling of what's coming next. "Your Honor, my client would like to change his plea."

"Mr. Jones, please stand. Is this true?"

"Yes, sir. I'd like to plead guilty."

The judge reads through the formalities, informing the defendant of his rights before he asks again. "Are you sure that you wish to plead guilty?"

"Yes, I want to plead guilty."

"The court will accept your plea. Your sentencing hearing will be at nine in the morning. Remand the defendant. Court dismissed." Well, that just made my day a lot shorter. I try to stay cool, calm and collected as I pack up and walk out, but I'm overjoyed. The case would be killing most hours of the day and I'd be lucky if I saw her more than just to pick her up from work.

As I hit the elevators, the defense attorney meets me there. He's in his sixties with a thick beard and a potbelly. He's looking pissed, and I'm not even sure why. Technically he didn't lose. His client realized that we had more against him than he could talk himself out of. "You're one hell of a smooth talker, but you better be careful because I'm not the kind of guy who likes to be shown up by a kid."

I stand to my full height, towering over him. Without raising my voice, I give him one warning, "Don't threaten me, grandpa. I'm not a fucking kid, and I'm not the kind of guy to piss off."

"I have friends—if you get my drift."

I chuckle, fixing my cuffs before adding, "I have friends and they call me Beast for a reason. Now, unless you want a formal complaint made against you, stay away from me." He takes a step back, and I get onto the elevator. Who the hell does that asshole think he is? I don't know, but I'm sure as fuck going to do my research.

In all my years, I've never had a lawyer outright threaten me before. It's almost comical that he thinks I'm that easy to intimidate. I give a call to Cyber, pulling in a favor. "Sure, I'll get everything on him by tomorrow."

"Good. Thanks."

When I walk into the bar, I hear Jackson ask, "And who are you?" My blood instantly boils, turning to the steam I swear is coming out of my ears. I don't give a fuck if he's the VP of the Steele Riders and Boomer's brother. I'll kick his fucking ass.

Boss answers, "This is Mary, my new hire."

"And off fucking limits," I snarl stalking toward the bar, giving Jackson a warning glare. Friend or not, if he makes a move, I'll butcher him. He's pulled up a seat next to his client who has him by the balls, but that doesn't ease my jealousy.

"Beast, beer?" Mary says, narrowing her eyes at me. She looks surprised to see me—pleasantly surprised.

"Yes, my sweet felony." Fucking, hell, I'm asking for trouble. A deep blush slips over her face. She's fucking beautiful with her long black hair in a thick braid hanging over her shoulder, looking good enough to eat. My cock throbs against my zipper. I'm glad I slipped on my suit jacket after getting out of my truck. The shape of my aching shaft would be on display otherwise.

"What are you doing here? It's only twelve." A level of suspicion crosses her face as she slides the beer to me. Does she think I don't trust her, and I'm checking up on her? I guess that's what I'm doing, but that's not why. I need my fix. I have to see her. More than that, I want to taste her. From head to toe, I want to lick every inch of Mary.

"He took a guilty plea," I answer, knowing I'm so guilty of lusting after my poor, sweet woman.

"That's awesome. Congrats." The bubbly way she says that goes straight to my balls. I picture coming home to tell her I've destroyed another defense and getting that sexy smile tossed my way. I'm holding the beer tighter than is smart, but I can't fight this hunger for her.

"Thanks." I take a long drink from the bottle and set it back on the bar. The distraction of Jackson who's in the middle of an argument with Penny helps me cool the burning need. I take the scene in and know that Jackson's got it bad for his client.

Penny and I haven't met officially, but now is not the right time to make introductions. From what I can see, Jackson's about to flip her ass over his shoulder. And yep, she's upside down and being carried out of the bar.

"Another one bites the dust," Boss says, chuckling and cleaning up their drinks from the bar.

"Absolutely." I turn back in my chair and stare at Mary. "How's it going?"

"It's okay. I'm not sure I'm cut out for this, but Boss has been sweet about it."

"Sweet?" I bite out, whipping my head toward Boss. He's drying some glasses, but he lifts his hands as if I've got a gun pointed at his ass.

"Relax, killer. She's old enough to be my kid."

She smiles at me, calming down the jealousy. Double-teamed, I relent and drink the rest of my beer.

"So, don't you have to spend more time on the next case?"

"Not yet. First, we have to get the sentencing phase of the trial over with and then I can set up the depositions this coming week, but I'm not going to trial for another month We have to check the calendar and schedule it. There's so much to do from one case to another and every defendant has their day in court, so the calendar can be really full."

"Nice." She fidgets, biting her bottom lip, waiting for me to say something else, but I can't stop staring at that mouth of hers. I miss kissing her.

Boss clears his throat and says, "Mary, can you wipe down the tables for me?"

"Yes, sir." She keeps her eyes on me, not moving for a few more seconds before pushing away and doing as Boss asked.

Boss looks at me and then leans down to whisper, "She's sweet and killer behind the bar. She's managed to learn most of the tricks in two days. She's not familiar with the cocktails, but the beer is all we really want her to handle right now. The only downside is how attractive she is." He watches my face, judging me and my motives. "Every red-blooded available man has tried to make a pass at her. I grumble something about her being my niece, which sends some of them running."

"Keep these fuckers away from her," I snarl, grinding my teeth so hard that I could swear I hear a crack. There's no denying that she's mine in my eyes even if I have to wait.

She comes back, and I slide my hand around her waist, pulling her so that her body is trapped between my legs as I sit on the stool. "Sweet Felony, I need to go and get some shit done, but I'll be back in a few hours."

"Okay." She looks away, focusing her attention on my suit jacket. I tip her chin to look up at me, seeing indecision in her eyes.

"Are you okay?" I ask with my voice gentle.

"Yes." She nods vigorously, and I don't believe her.

"Am I pushing you too far?" I don't want to overwhelm her with my crazy possessiveness.

"No, but you know we have to keep our distance."

"I understand, but I can't stop stealing just a touch." It hits me hard that I'm the one who can't act like an adult in this situation. I have no damn self-control, and it's disappointing.

"See ya later, Beast." She pushes away from me and moves behind the bar, wiping her hands off on the bar towel. I take one last look at her as she works, but she doesn't lift her head up, so I get up to leave, and as usual, I peek through the reflection to take in her beauty one more time without her knowing.

I step out into the sunshine and feel a sense of emptiness. My phone rings and I see it's Spencer. As soon as I'm in my SUV, I hook it up to my vehicle's Bluetooth. "What's going on, Charles?"

"I'm seeing how it's going."

"It's fine. What else? I know you're not calling just for that."

"Serrano got the judge to release him on bail."

"What?" I roar, braking too hard, causing eyes to land on mine. I pull off to the side, parking in front of the local grocery store.

"He's getting out today. He'll still have a monitor on him, so it's not like he can get to her, but I wanted to give you a heads up."

"Fucking shitty judges," I grumble. Clearing my throat that suddenly feels like a frog is stuck in it, I say, "Fine. I'll keep her protected."

"I knew you would. Talk to you later." He ends the call, and I slam my head against the headrest.

Boomer sends out a text reminding everyone that we're having a get together at the clubhouse tonight. Riders and family only. I get a second text from Boomer. ***You know Mary's welcome as well.***

I want her to come, but at the same time, I don't. There are way too many prospects that'll be there that are her age or slightly older. I'll end up killing one of them if they even flirt with her, but I have to go because I need to talk with the guys about Serrano.

I prepare for the party with my vest on, wanting to bring Mary with me, but there'll be too many questions about her background and our relationship that I can't answer.

When I come out of the bedroom, I see Mary reading. I don't want to interrupt her, but I can't go without saying goodbye. "Mary, I'm out. I'll be back later. Don't wait up for me and don't try to leave. I'm going to lock down the house." I haven't told her about Serrano because she doesn't need the extra paranoia. Instead, I turn and walk out without waiting for her to reply.

I feel like a total dick for leaving without her. As soon as I pull into the clubhouse, I'm beyond irritated at myself and at her. Why did she have to come in and fuck up my world by being everything I could ever want and someone I can't have.

Sensing my mood, Wrench hands me a beer. I don't even wait to polish off the bottle. I toss it in the recycling bin and then go grab another. It's going to be a long and miserable night.

"Slow down, or you'll be smashed before everyone gets here."

"I'm fine. Don't worry about me," I mutter, finishing another. All I can think about is what Mary's doing right now. Does she hate me for not bringing her? Probably.

Chapter Seven

Mary

THE DAY WENT FROM WONDERFUL TO TERRIBLE. WHEN Beast showed up at the bar, I had to change my panties, and when he pulled me into my arms, I knew they were ruined. Now, I'm watching him drive away to a party that I'm not welcome at. My heart feels like it's in my stomach as I think about what he's doing without me.

I've heard and read what happens at parties like this with a bunch of bikers. They have a lot of names for the women who come to fuck the bikers for beer and more. I want to throat punch any clubhouse whore who comes near Beast. He's supposed to be mine. Although, today I pushed him away, reminding him that we can't be together and leaving him available to every slut around. God, I feel like shit. My stomach churns as I picture him banging one of these bitches on the side of the clubhouse or in his SUV.

"Whatever. Get a hold of yourself. You're not in love

with him." I shout out the words, but I know that they're nothing but lies. No matter what I tell myself, I've gone off the deep end. I've fallen for Beast, and it hurts to the depths of my soul that he can just detach himself from me and bang anything that walks.

I continue to mope around the house, avoiding the kitchen because as silly as it seems, I feel like it's where he and I became something more than just a handler and his assignment.

Hours pass by, and I'm home alone. I can't stop thinking about how hot he looked when he slipped on that Steele Rider vest. I had to dry my lips and change my panties. It's so sexy the way he goes from hard as stone, don't mess with me DA to this dark, Beastlike biker in his fully patched up vest. My body forgets for a moment that I'm upset, and I crave his hands on mine all over again.

I lay back on the sofa, turn on the television with a large bowl of popcorn, and put on a romantic comedy. By the end of the movie, I hear Beast pulling into the gate. I click it off and clean up my mess before he makes it to the door. He opens the door to see me washing the bowl I used. He's a little tipsy, but there's something in his eyes that screams regret. I refuse to ask why because I don't want to know that he's been with someone tonight.

"You're still up," he sighs as if he hoped I'd be asleep already. I wonder if there's a woman by the front door waiting to sneak in his room. I know the party is probably for more than the Riders, and he's just itching to hook up with the easy bitches that show up for men like him.

I shove him away. Maybe it's for the best. "I don't have a bedtime. Excuse me," I say as I push past him. I get the faint whiff of perfume off his clothes, answering my own question. "Goodnight." It's the only thing I can say without breaking into tears.

"Goodnight, Sweet Felony." The strong stench of booze hits my nose, and I'm too pissed to even think straight.

"The name is Mary." I storm into my room and slam the door. I can't take this any longer. I really have to figure out what's going to happen. I didn't see anyone at the front door or in the living room, but that probably means he already nailed the bitch at the clubhouse.

"Mary? What's wrong?" I hear the thud of his forehead pressing on the door.

"Nothing. You're drunk. Go to bed." I walk into the guest bathroom and close the door loud enough for him to hear and maybe get the hint to leave me alone. I get ready for bed, washing away the tears that have stained my face.

For the next hour, I sit on my bed, thinking about how I'm going to make it through the day and how I'm going to be able to even see Beast without losing it. I pick up my suitcase and flip it on the bed. Loading it up with my clothes, I stop and try to figure out how I can get away without Beast knowing. I sit on the bed and grab my phone. I can't contact my former co-workers because it's too dangerous. Twirling it in my hands, I wonder if it's a smart idea to call Detective Spencer.

It takes me another ten minutes before I build up the nerve to call.

"Hello?" His voice is hoarse from sleep, and I feel like a jerk for waking him up.

"Detective Spencer, sorry to bother you. I forgot it was so late. I'm wondering and I know this is a huge deal, but is there a way you could move me somewhere else?" I get that what I'm doing is rash, but I have to get away from him before I get any deeper. Hell, I'm already too deep, but I can't handle the heartache that's going to come.

"Why? Is something wrong there?"

I sigh because I hadn't thought of a reason for such a logical question. "It's complicated. Let's just say that I don't feel safe here." My heart's the only thing that's not safe here. *I hate Beast—that bastard.* Do they fuck the women and pass them around? Eww. I'm so damn disgusted that I can't think straight.

"Okay. I'll come and get you first thing in the morning."

"Can you be here at ten? That's when he's going to be gone." He's supposed to do something with Boomer. I know that because he told me when he picked me up from work last night. It's probably my only way out.

"Sure. I'll move you somewhere safe," he says a little clearer than before, but I'm sure he's ready to go back to bed. "Be waiting in the front yard for me."

"I will. Goodnight." I hang up and then finish packing my bags before setting them aside.

I set the alarm on my phone and pass out for the night

I'm grateful I packed my things last night because I woke up late. Apparently, I set the alarm for nine PM instead of AM. I look at my watch, I see it's almost ten in the morning. Using the bathroom and brushing my teeth, I do one last look over the room to see if I'm missing anything.

Once I'm sure, I step out of the room and peek out the window. I see that Beast has already left, making it easy for me to get out of the house undetected. With my two bags over my shoulder and my suitcase handle in my left hand, I walk down the stairs and move toward the front. It feels like the longest walk ever. Maybe it's because I'm worried that Beast is going to stop me or maybe because I hope he does. "Stay strong. You can do this," I mutter.

I'm almost to the iron gate when a hand steels around my waist, and another hand slides around my mouth with something strong-smelling in it. I fight, kick, and scream, but it doesn't work, and I'm quickly losing steam. Suddenly, everything begins to go dark.

Chapter Eight

Beast

I WAKE UP GROGGY AND FEELING LIKE SHIT, BUT NOT because I drank a lot. No, because I gave Mary the wrong impression. Before I could explain what happened, she smelled the body spray Morgan accidentally got me with last night. The reason I drank too much is partly my feelings for Mary, but also Serrano, the man she was about to testify against was released on bond. I'm sure he could easily find a way to come after Mary, ankle monitor or not.

Once I'm fully awake, I can hear her rustling around in the house. I check my phone, and I see a message from Spencer, alerting me that Mary wants to be picked up and he's on his way.

"Over my dead body," I growl out, slipping on some clothes quietly to stop her from going. The thud of her suitcase hits the floor, and then I hear my silent alarm. She's left the house, but that's not her who tripped the silent alarm. It's coming from my gate. Shit. I grab my gun from my holster and run outside just in time to see some bastard wrap his arms around her, one on her face. I'm outside in a second because the stupid fuck is weak and doesn't realize her weight is going to be heavier now that she's passed out. As she falls to the ground, I aim right at the fucker, putting a bullet in his chest.

I'm down to them in a few steps, scooping her up in my arms and kicking the fucker onto his back. I'm not surprised that it's Serrano, but he's surprised to see me as he gasps for air. The stupid piece of shit won't have time for the medics to arrive. "You touched my wife. Now you pay."

Carrying Mary back into the house, I set her on the sofa. From the smell on her face, I know he's given her a strong dose of Chloroform. I have to get her a washcloth and try to put it on her head while getting Doc over here as soon as possible. Needing to get this dead body out of my front lawn, I call Law. "Hey, I have a dead son of a bitch in my front lawn. It's a legal shoot, but I need you."

"Understood." He knows that if I wanted to make this go away without the cops, I would call Boomer to get the Riders over here, but he's fled the jurisdiction and committed several other crimes the second he stepped onto my property. Just minutes later, Spencer pulls up to my front gate. I want to kick his ass for letting Mary think that she could get away from me, but all that matters is she's safe where she belongs.

"Wow, holy shit!" he hollers, jumping out of his car

and staring at the body on the ground. I open my gate and let him in to help me with this bastard. He moves closer and examines Serrano, who's dead. "You nailed that fucker. I guess there's no trial needed, but I have to call it in."

"Go ahead. The Steeleville Sheriff is on his way right now."

"Where's Mary?" He's not taking her from me no matter what she told him. I'm not letting her out of my sight.

"In the house. I need to get back to her."

"Please tell me she's okay." He says it, but he's busy looking down at Serrano and checking him for weapons.

"He drugged her and tried to take her out of here. I think he wanted her to end up missing unable to testify," I add as we both stare at the dead body.

"There's no doubt about that. Shit. I have to call my superiors." Spencer makes a call to his boss. It's not the ending the family would have liked, but I'm not concerned about them. All I care about is my woman in the house. As much as I want to go in there and comfort her, I don't want to leave the body until my guy gets here. Thankfully, I hear Law's sirens blare, and then twenty seconds later, he pulls into my open gate.

He jumps out with one of his deputies who pulls out a crime scene camera. "Wow, this guy's mug is all over the news. He's either stupid or desperate," Law says, examining the clean through and through in his chest.

"He almost had her." The shock of it still registering.

"Go ahead and take care of her." I run inside the

house and bring a fresh, wet washcloth to her head. "Mary, my sweet felony, please wake up for me."

She cries out, slowly gaining her wits when she freaks out on me. Her beautiful bright eyes are full of fear. "You attacked me! Please leave me alone." She shoves at my chest but she's not strong enough to make me budge.

I shake my head, brushing her hair behind her ear. "Baby, I didn't. You didn't see him then, did you?" She flinches from my touch which hurts more than it should.

"See who? You tricked me, making me think you left. Were you listening to my conversation?"

"I get that you're mad at me, but you better calm your ass down. You acting rashly this morning had some serious consequences." I grab her hand and lift her to her feet. She's weak and wobbly, so I hold onto her tight. "If you don't believe me, you can see for yourself." I picked her up and set her down to stand in the front door where Law is laying a sheet over the body.

I don't hide the image from her because she needed to understand that I'm the one who will always protect her and slay her dragons. "That's Serrano. He came to get you. He must have thought I left like you did." I'm being a dick, but she's got me fucking losing my mind.

"Thank you." She turns and wrenches herself free from my arms. "Now that he's dead, can I go home?"

"This is your home." She's about to argue when up walk Law and Spencer.

"Can we come in?" Law asks, and he's not looking at me for approval. This doesn't have anything to do with my need for solitude. Instead, he's wondering if Mary's okay with it. She nods only, refusing to speak.

"Of course." I step out of the doorway and then close it so Mary can't sneak out again.

"Mary, I'm so glad you're safe, but if you're up to it, I need to ask you some questions."

"I need to get Doc here," I inform them. She needs to be evaluated whether she likes it or not.

"I sent him a message while we were outside," Law adds. I mouthed a silent thank you to him.

"So, can you tell me about what happened?" Law continues. Since this is his jurisdiction, he's ranking officer.

"I thought Serrano was supposed to be in jail not out here ready to nab me the second I step outside." She glares at Spencer.

"I'm sorry. I called Beast yesterday and let him know."

"Well, he was too busy getting lucky to let me know." Spencer and Law give us questioning looks.

"Not now, Mary," I snarl at her, ready to bend her over and spank her foolish ass. Turning to Law, I start talking, "I woke up to Mary moving around. After I saw your message, I knew she was waiting for you, so I dressed quickly and then I heard her leave. I was almost out the door when I saw Serrano grab her. Unable to hold her weight, he stumbled with her in his arms. Once he stood up, I took my shot. He was on my property trying to get rid of the only witness to a murder that can send him away forever."

"Yes, stand your ground definitely fits this case, especially since he's violated the conditions of his bail."

"That it does," Law mutters. We can hear several sirens in the background. "It should be the Ellis County coroner's office and CSI," Law says.

"We'll meet with them. Stay inside for now until the doctor has evaluated her," Spencer says, standing up and walking outside with Law following behind him.

I reach out for Mary, but she pulls away. "Look, I didn't fuck anyone yesterday. I shouldn't have gotten so shitfaced, but the thought of not being able to have you frustrated me."

"So, you didn't fuck her, but you must have…" She's thinking about other intimate things in that pretty little head of hers, but I can't let her think any of it because it's the furthest thing from the truth.

"I didn't do anything but drink. The perfume you smelled was an accidental spray on me from Morgan. She was showing Crystal a new body spray, or some shit she bought when I barreled past them to leave." She gives me a suspicious but hopeful gaze. My sweet felony wants to believe me, but I guess I didn't make the best decisions last night. "I owe you an apology for not bringing you with last night."

"No. You don't owe me anything. I don't have to be around your friends."

"I didn't want you there until you were mine. If you were mine, then I could drag you everywhere telling everyone that you belong to me. There are way too many single Riders and prospects, some much closer in age to you. There's no way I wouldn't beat someone's ass if they flirted with you."

Her face blushes, and then she moves to stand but loses her balance. "I'm here to catch you. I'll always be," I say, holding her in my arms. Sitting Mary on my lap, I run my hands over her face. I put the back of my hand to her forehead, checking her temperature. She's not too hot.

"I see you're playing doctor," Doc teases from the door.

"Well, since someone's ass took forever, I decided to play doctor. She nearly fainted," I grumble. I'm in a better mood now that I got that misunderstanding out of the way, but there's a serious fucking issue here in front of us. A dead body on my lawn. A body that had been touching my woman's body.

"Mary, this is Doc or as he's professionally known as Dr. Joseph Simmons."

"Hello, Mary. I'm sorry about what happened, but I need to check a few things?"

"Okay." He pulls out the penlight gadget and opens her eyelids to check her pupils.

"How are you feeling? Do you have a headache, nausea, dizziness?"

"A bit of all of that." He uses a scanning thermometer on her forehead. It beeps with a red mark appearing on the screen.

"You have a slight fever. It's probably because of the rag he put over your face. I gave a cursory examination of his person and found a squirt bottle full of chloroform in his pocket. The side effects should pass after the next day, but I'd recommend: food, rest and plenty of fluids. And Beast, if you have some pain meds, that would be helpful. I'd say Tylenol because Ibuprofen causes stomach irritation, and she's already feeling nauseous." He pats her leg and then stands up.

"Thank you, Doc," Mary and I say at the same time.

"It's what I do. Now, if you don't have meds let me know and I'll bring some back."

"I've got a bottle of Tylenol in the bathroom," I say.

"Yeah, and did you take some for yourself? You drank like I've never seen before."

"Well, about that. My truck is still at the clubhouse."

"Actually, I drove it here. Law's going to give me a ride back, so here are your keys."

"Thanks, brother."

"That's what we're here for."

Mary lays her head on my chest, and I snuggle her close. She's so much smaller than me that I can easily carry her to our bedroom. No more sleeping alone. "Um. Wrong room."

"No, it's not. We're not going to fuck yet, but if you think I want to spend another night alone, you're wrong. I want to hold you as soon as I get some food and fluids inside you."

"That sounded so dirty."

"Well, those fluids will be filling you up soon—very soon. Rest. I'll be back in a few minutes with something to drink and some meds."

Chapter Nine

Mary

I FELL ASLEEP RIGHT AFTER HE GAVE ME THE MEDS AND water, but I'm not sure how long I've been asleep, and I'm afraid to find out.

My body aches. It takes me a minute to remember that Serrano dropped me after he knocked me out. I look toward the window and see it's dark out and I'm in Beast's bed. Shit. All my drama and self-torture was for nothing. I can't believe I let myself almost be kidnapped and murdered. I feel like such a twat. I'm so grateful Beast, my Beast, came to my rescue.

The door opens, and I look up and see the most ridiculously hot sight. Beast is in just a pair of gray joggers, his chest's bare and is almost as wide as the doorframe. I stare at the small dark tuff of hair that goes from his sculpted chest down below his sexy grey sweats. Seriously, I can't stop staring at his package. It's not very well wrapped at the moment and I crave his touch—I might have missed out on this forever.

When the truth finally hits me, the emotions are too much. My body shakes uncontrollably, knowing that a minute difference and I'd be dead already. I would have never been able to see Beast again.

"You're up," he says with a smile stretching across his face, which shifts when he notices my state. He's on the bed and dragging me onto his lap in a flash. I feel so safe and so foolish.

"I'm sorry, baby. I'm sorry." He rocks me as if I'm a child.

I reach my hand up and press it to his strong, scruffy cheek. "I'm the sorry one. I could have died today and never seen you again." Tears stream down my face worse than they had yesterday.

"Shh, shh. Don't think like that. Think about you being here with me forever because that's where you belong."

"Forever?" I question. It's supposed to be temporary, and now that Serrano's gone, I'm safe to go back to my apartment.

"I love you, Mary."

His muscles coil around me, holding me tight. Beast's lips press to my temple in the gentlest way. I love the tenderness he gives to me. No words are spoken or needed.

We stay like this until my stomach reminds us that I haven't eaten today.

"Shit, okay. Let me get you some food."

"What time is it?"

"Five."

"I slept for five hours," I exclaim, trying to get up, but he gently pulls me back down.

"Yes, but you needed it. You still need it."

"Thanks." I slide off of him, and he stands up. When he sees me on my feet, he shakes his head. "Lay back down."

"No. I'm going to sit up and eat."

"Fine." He grabs me around the waist and under my knees, scooping me up in his brawny arms, carrying me to the kitchen and then settling me down on the counter. "Not the way I imagined you on this surface. The only crying I was hoping for is my name off your lips as I fucking devour your pussy."

"Wow, um…well…I'm already up here," I offer, parting my thighs.

He moves to stand between my legs and growls, crushing his mouth to mine. "As much as I'd love that, you're not ready. Today has been hell, and you need to eat something."

I run my hands over his chest, threading my fingers through his dark hairs. "A plain sandwich will do just fine." I don't want him to go through so much trouble for me, especially after he already killed a man for me today. Although I use the word man loosely.

"Ha. A plain sandwich for my woman? I think not," he scoffs, pretending to be offended. I love the light in his eyes. It's the first time I've truly seen him smile with all his face.

I giggle at the silliness. "You're ridiculous."

"You haven't even seen the half of it." He nuzzles my neck and the giggles turn into moans. My hands cling to his hips, grasping the waistband of his joggers. They're just a tug away from coming off and I want them down so I can see that thick cock he's doing nothing to hide. "Oh, no. Should I try running again?"

He stops looks up at me like I'm crazy. "No. I'm not sure you understand what I'll do to keep you by my side," he adds, dipping his head back to my neck and jaw.

"I know you're capable of killing a man to protect me," I say through sighs.

"I'd kill a hundred if they even looked at you funny." He kisses me hard, stealing my breath and my heart.

I shove him back just a bit. "Sounds like a bit much."

"Well, call me crazily obsessed, but I'd do much more if it meant you were always safe." He takes my mouth again, sliding his tongue over mine. He pulls off and tips his head back to look at me. "We're not done, but you need to eat." He slips his hand between us and cups my pussy, and then growls, "And then I need to eat." His intent clear, and my panties soaked.

He moves away and starts to cook. I don't know what he's planning to make me, but we've been cooking for each other since I arrived. When I see he has the cheese and bread with tomato, my mouth waters. He's making me a fancy and delicious grilled cheese. While his back is turned, I shimmy my shorts off my legs. I'm not bold enough to take my panties off, but I want him to keep his promise. I don't want to stop until he has me pinned with his cock buried deep inside of me.

His back stiffens, but he doesn't turn around. My beast can't hide that he's well aware that my shorts are on the floor. I watch his muscles move as he cooks for me. Damn, they are so lickable. I start rubbing my chest, feeling overheated. My fingers graze over my hardened nipples, and I hiss. Pure desire shoots down between my legs. I stare at his ass, biting my lip and squeezing my legs closed. My hands roam over my body, scraping my tender peaks over the cotton of his tee and down lower.

A moan escapes my lips and then I hear him grunt. "You're food is done." He turns off the stove and then grabs the plate. Spinning around on his heels, we make eye contact. "Enough touching yourself. It's my job." I don't remove my hands because I want him to do it for me. He sets the plate on the counter next to me and moves between my legs. "Tell me, Mary. What should I do to your pretty, sexy little ass because you don't listen to me?" He presses his hand over mine, controlling it as he pushes two of my fingers against my slit. My panties are providing that extra friction and I'm almost about to come and then he stops, grips my hand hard, and wraps it behind my back. With his free hand, he picks up the sandwich and brings it to my mouth. "Take a bite of your food, or I'm not going to let you come."

I bite down, and he pulls it away as the cheese stretches between my lips and the sandwich. I swipe my tongue around and then biting off the rest of the gooey cheese. Never has a grilled cheese ever tasted so good. He sets it down and then cups my face and kisses me.

"Sweet felony, I'm going to make you come and then I'm going to take you to our bed and fill you with my baby." He lifts the sandwich and makes me take another bite. As I chew, he skims his hands up my legs, sending jolts of electricity through me. Inch by inch, he kisses his way toward my pussy. I toss my head back. He stops and growls, "Another bite."

I follow his command, taking one more bite. He grabs the hem of my panties and drags them down my body, tossing them backward.

"Somebody is dirtying their kitchen. I can't believe you would do that."

"I'd trash this whole fucking place if it meant I could worship your sexy body." He kisses my mound, brushing his nose against it, and inhales. "Fuck, you smell fantastic." His tongue swipes across my folds before he pushes inward. I lose my mind, coming on the spot. Shaking and throbbing, I scream his name. Beast doesn't stop until every drop of me is on him. I'm boneless as I lean on my elbows, panting. Damn, who knew getting an orgasm could make you tired? I always heard the men fall asleep afterward. I guess because most talk about a woman not coming, but the man is going to have me sleeping all day with that mouth of his.

He stands and I think he's going to take me right there, but instead, he adjusts himself and starts putting the dishes in the sink. "Come on, time to finish your meal and then off to bed."

"What? I thought we were going to—you know…"

"As much as I want to drill your sweet pussy, I want you well-fed and rested."

"Well, my pussy's hungry and wants to be fed."

"Damn it, woman. I'm trying to be a gentleman." His teeth bite into his bottom lip.

My hand creeps between us and grabs his cock through his sweats. Leaning in, I nip at his scruffy jaw and whisper, "Leave him at the office. I want the biker. Time to feed the Beast."

In one swoop, I'm upside down over his shoulder and being carried out of the kitchen. As he marches me through the house, I watch his ass flex and bounce with every step. Men can have really sexy asses, and Beast has got a killer one. I smack it, giggling when he grunts. As soon as we get in the room, he sets the plate on the nightstand and then flips me onto the mattress. I bust out in laughter when I spot my half-eaten sandwich. "I can't believe you brought my food with."

"Just in case you get a little weak on me, my dear. I want you passing out from orgasms not starvation." He drops his joggers to his feet, stepping out of them without another word. He's completely naked. I thought his dick was huge, but I was wrong; it's fucking massive and thick. It stands on its own, like a damn flagpole. I slip my tongue out and lick my suddenly parched lips. "Keep that up and I'm going to be feeding your mouth first."

"I like that." I move to my knees and crawl to the edge of the bed. Kneeling, our mouths are at the same height, and he kisses me roughly, letting me taste my own passion. His hand spears through my hair, cupping the back of my head and dragging me as close to him as possible. Moaning and running my hands over his broad shoulders, I need more and reach for his thick cock, but he's not having that and I'm on my back before I can touch shaft.

Chapter Ten

Beast

I flip my woman onto her back. As much as I want her mouth wrapped around my cock, I'm so close that I'll come before she slides it to the back of her throat. I've never been this hard in my entire life. She's got me so wound up I can't even think straight. "I want you coming on my tongue again before I take your pussy."

She moans, flexing her hips and pouting sexily. Grabbing hold of her tiny waist with both of my meaty hands, engulfing her frame, turns me on. I'm so much larger than her that I'm going to break her in half, and I want to do it as she comes while I'm deep inside her. Sliding down her body, I nestle myself between her thighs and my head in front of my feast.

I swipe my lips over her slit, tasting her sweet core. Her body shakes with every thrust of my tongue between her folds. She moans, rolling her hips up to my mouth. The way she comes apart from my touch causes my cock to dribble come onto the sheets. Shit. I'm so hard that I'm going to drill a hole through the mattress with my dick.

Her hands thrust into my hair, dragging her fingers over my scalp. I ache for her cries that slip past her lips. "Come for me, my sweet felony. I want to hear you one more time before I fill you up."

"William." She clenches her thighs around my head, sealing me in while she comes hard on my face. I lap up every drop until she relaxes her hold. It's the first time she shouts my name, and the sound of it from her lips almost makes me come.

"Say it again," I growl against her mound.

"William." My dick jerks again, staying rock hard. I climb up her body, needing to finally fill her up. I push the head inside merely an inch, taking my time before I come too soon.

"I'm ready to be yours."

"You've been mine since the day we met." I dip my head and slip my tongue into her mouth. Needing to move so badly, I give in and roll my hips forward, stuffing my cock deep in her pussy shredding through the hints of her innocence.

She lets out a whimper, and I groan, hating that I caused her an ounce of pain. Our eyes meet and I see the answer to the unasked question. She gave me her virginity. I can't believe she didn't tell me, but I'm not complaining. In fact, I'm mentally celebrating. Until I met her, I've never felt possessive, but I can't even think of her with another man or I'll lose my mind.

"You're mine. Only mine until the day I die." I don't move inside, but I'm not ready to stop. Time stands still as we stare at each other, longing and promise in both our eyes. Taking it slow, I kiss and lick my way to her breasts, sucking her hard nipples into my mouth one at a time until she's moaning, and her pussy squeezes my cock even harder than the vice grip it had already. Steeling my hands into her hair, I take her lips, kissing her the way I crave, delving inside her mouth and letting our tongues dance.

Her hands slide over my shoulders and down my back. "William, please."

"Are you ready for me?" I drag my lips along her chest, sucking on her perfect tits. "I love your breasts. I can't wait until they're filled with my baby's meals. Do you want to have my baby?"

"Yes." Her walls flex around my cock.

I know she's turned on almost as much as I am about having my baby. "Do you want my seed?" She nods, but I have to hear it from her lips. "Tell me. Say it, and I'll give you every damn drop."

Her lip quivers as she throatily moans. "Yes, I want your seed."

"You're going to get it all." Finally, I give in to the pleasure and begin thrusting in and out of her tight core and watch as she comes apart in my arms. I skim my hands up and down her sides, halting at her hips and lifting them to drive deeper. She grips onto my forearms for support as I fuck her tight womb.

"I'm coming. Oh, William, so deep." Her cries send

me over the edge, jetting come into her cunt, filling her belly.

Still buried in her, I drop head to the side on the mattress.

"Oh my God, that was incredible. I want to do it again."

"I hope so, sweetheart, because this is for life. You're mine." I managed to say feeling thoroughly pleased and winded at the same time.

"I meant right now."

"I'd love to, but I need to get you another snack or something. I don't think the sandwich is good anymore."

"Too bad because it's so delicious."

"But then again, so were you." I flip her onto her back and take her again.

"I started a bath for you. I'm sure you could use it to soothe all your sore parts." I wink at her, trying to tease.

"Thank you. I could definitely use it. Someone's massive cock and brawny body savaged me."

"Damn right. You created that savage. You created that monster."

"No, I unleashed the Beast."

"Keep that shit up, and you'll never make it out of this bed." I crawl over her, grinding my hips so she can feel how hard I am. She lifts her hands, sliding them across my jaw and then into my hair. Dragging me down for a kiss, I willingly surrender.

The sound of water hitting the bathroom floor forces us apart. "Shit."

"I'll just take a shower in the other bathroom."

"Good idea."

Chapter Eleven

Beast

It's Monday, and I hated leaving Mary, but I still have a job and a lot of questions to answer when it comes to the death of Serrano. When I step out of my vehicle, I'm greeted by the press, shouting questions my way.

I should have expected it. Shit. Taking a beat, I stop by the entrance and turn to address them. "The event that took place this Saturday was unfortunate; however, I defended my home and my fiancée. Who he is and where he came from hadn't crossed my mind when he crossed my lawn. His death was caused by his choices. Learning he was the man who my fiancée planned to testify against made the incident a little more unnerving, but she's safe."

"How is your fiancée?"

"She's recovering both physically and emotionally.

Thank you. Please excuse me. I still have cases to work on."

I excuse myself and walk inside the building out of sight of the cameras. Francisco is waiting at the elevators the second I step off of them.

"Sir, I'm glad to hear you're okay. The Dallas County DA on the Serrano case is waiting for you. I put him in conference room A. I already grabbed him some coffee."

"Good. Thanks. Can you grab me a cup of coffee?" He nods, and I add, "I'll be in with him after I set my things down." It only takes me a minute or two to prepare myself for this meeting. I don't have time for this, but it has to be done. It's not as if I'm the average guy. This is a big deal because the public is worried that I'm a target. Frankly, I know I am. It sucks, but if there's any of Serrano's associates or family looking for revenge, I'm the one they are coming for. Unfortunately for them, I'm well equipped to destroy anyone who gets in my way. My guys already informed me that they have my back should we need to remove some bodies, but I don't want it to come to that.

As I exit my office, Francisco holds out my mug for me to take. "Thank you." I nod and head into the conference room.

I enter the room and the DA stands immediately. He's alone which means that he doesn't want this conversation to go beyond these walls for the time being. "Hello, I'm DA Moses Madden. I'm sorry for this impromptu meeting."

"I expected no less." We shake hands, and he sits back down.

I take my seat. "So, what happens now?"

"Nothing. His death was listed as a *stand your ground* matter. I'm only here to answer any questions you have."

"I have a bunch. How the fuck did he find out where I live? And most importantly, how did he know when to strike?"

"That's something we're looking into. Spencer informed us that he got a call from Ms. Stark. She's not supposed to contact him, so I'm guessing someone tapped into his phone and listened to the call. We're checking because it wasn't a secure line, so it's not hard to do. How he got your address could be a location software he used."

"I've got another question. Is there someone out there that cares if he's dead?"

"Like most of us, there's at least one person, but his ties to the drug world are great. He wasn't some petty criminal or a hitman. Although someone might send you a gift basket now that he's gone."

"Why? Did he plan to rat anyone out?"

"Not that we were aware of, but you know the risks when one is caught. They usually don't want to go down alone. We're going through it all to make sure he doesn't have associates involved in this. If he had accomplices in this attack, they could be looking to finish the job, so letting down your guard may not be the best thing for you or Ms. Stark."

"Son of a bitch." I slam my hands on the table.

"I'm sorry, but this thing with Serrano was bigger

than Spencer led on. Ms. Stark's witness testimony would help bring a trafficking empire to its knees. You weren't only chosen because you were a safe bet, but because we know the Steele Riders are very protective of their town, which has its own rights and laws."

"That makes sense. So Spencer's a dickhead for leaving out the rest. I get the need for it, but my guard would have been higher up if I'd known. Excuse me, I need to make a call."

I stand and leave to make a call to Boomer. "Hey, I need more security at my house and around Mary."

"Already on it. After what I heard, I've talked to Cyber. We're doing all we can from our end. Is there something else?"

"Yes, Serrano wasn't just a small-time dealer getting caught in the commission of a drug murder. He worked for a drug trafficking cartel."

"Are you thinking Cortes?"

"I don't know, but I'm guessing the fuck so. The DA and Spencer are holding everything tight to the vest. I'm guessing a rat on the inside."

"I agree. We'll do what we can on our end. You know I want Cortes not only shutdown but at the end of my barrel."

"We'll hold our cards tight to the chest as well."

"Okay. Good. It's time we go to church. Tonight."

"Understood. Are you going to bring the girls?"

"Yes."

"Good. I'll bring Mary."

"It's official now?"

"Damn right. I made sure of it. There's no need for

me to pretend it isn't anymore. The bastard is in the morgue, and her part of the case is all gone. Now, if they want to fuck with me, I'll send more bodies to the morgue."

"We got your back, brother."

"Thanks. I need to get back to my meeting, but I just had to call you for this."

"Anytime."

When I walk back into the meeting, a man and a woman have joined the DA around the table. They aren't dressed professionally, so I'm already guessing these are the victim's parents.

"Sorry, DA Brandon. Mr. and Mrs. Gates wanted to come and speak with you."

"We'd just like to say thank you. Although we wanted to see him rot in prison, we know you didn't have a choice."

"Thank you for understanding. This situation was completely out of my control, and the only solution was his death."

"He's not the only one involved though. We came here because a couple of guys showed up at our house, looking for something. They had their faces covered, so we can't identify them, but they roughed up my husband and demanded to know where Shawn's bedroom was. They ransacked the place and left. We don't know what they took or who they were, but I'm guessing they know he had something important."

I drop back in my chair and think about all the information I was given in that meeting. It lasted another half an hour before they took their leave. Francisco walked them out, and I went into my office, feeling completely off-kilter.

It's been hours since I talked to Mary. Is that what's wrong with me? I need my woman to ease some of this tension. Nothing they told me was truly new to me. I had suspected it, and they verified my worst fears.

The phone only rings once before she answers. I release a breath I hadn't realized I was holding.

"Hey, babe. How's it going?"

"I saw you on the news today. The whole fiancée thing really sells what you did out here Saturday."

"It's not selling shit. I haven't gotten your ring yet, but I'm sure it's a done deal. You're going to marry me soon."

"Oh, really? No need to ask?"

"Why? When I already know the answer."

"A man of few words."

"So how's your day," I ask, ignoring her original question. I love to know what's going on with her. She's supposed to spend a quiet day, filling up her Kindle Crystal bought her. I gave her my credit card and let her go hog wild with it. I'd pay anything to see that beautiful smile on her face.

"So far, all I did was clean and shower. I don't have a lot of clothes, so laundry's a must."

"I'll take you out this weekend, and you can pick a whole bunch of things including stuff for a wedding."

"Oh yeah, and when is this wedding taking place?"

"As soon as I can con you into doing it."

"I'd say it's going to take a lot more orgasms for me

to be convinced into marrying the sexiest, toughest man who saves me like a damsel in distress all the time."

"I'll eat your pussy until you pass out. If I didn't have to work, I'd be working on your third at the very least."

"Confident, aren't we?"

"With you, fuck yeah. Nothing is sexier to me than the sound of your screams."

"Um...are you trying to phone sex me, *DA Brandon*?"

"No, you get me so damn worked up, my cock is thinking it's a sex session. Did you buy any books yet?"

"Only one right now. I'm halfway through with it, but some hot guy called, and I had to answer because I'm sure he'd break down the door if I didn't."

"I have the key, but you're damn right I would leave the damn courtroom if you didn't answer, baby. You are my number one priority."

"Thank you, William. I love you."

"I love it when you call me by my name. I've never really noticed it before, but the way it comes off your lips makes it ten times better."

"Well then, Mr. Brandon, when you get home, I'll make sure that I whisper it, chant it, scream it. All. Night. Long."

"Fucking shit, you're going to make me whip my dick out right here in my office and beat off to the visions I'm having right now."

"Oh, don't do that. I'd be jealous of any female in your office who heard that deep, rugged moan that comes from the back of your throat when you're close to coming."

"I'm hanging up. When I get home, I'm bending you

over and punishing you for that." I end the call to a fit of giggles from her end of the line. The brat. She's going to get me in trouble for indecent exposure. I have another meeting in ten minutes, and I have to get my cock under control before someone sues for sexual harassment.

I head into my small bathroom and pour some cold water over my face and wet a paper towel to put on my cock. It does the trick long enough for it to go down. Grabbing what I need for my next meeting, I walk out and step into conference room B, where the detectives are here to go over a homicide involving a jilted lover and a wife.

Chapter Twelve

Mary

I TAKE A DRINK OF COFFEE AND TURN ON THE NEWS TO see if anyone mentions the incident with Serrano. The first thing I see is William's handsome face. He's walking from his SUV to the building past all the reporters that gathered. They're shouting questions, and he appears extremely annoyed. I want to smack them and tell them to leave him alone.

The ramifications could be great from the attack, but he handles the situation like it's all said and done, and everyone can go about their day. Maybe that is the case. Maybe there are more people than just me and the victim's family that are pleased that Serrano's dead. I've never been the vengeful type in my life, especially after the hand that I'd been dealt, but his death brings me a newfound sense of peace.

It does help that I have one hell of a man watching my six at all times. I think about the way he's allowed me to just engulf his space, and it makes me feel at home. The way he loves me so much that I can't get enough of it.

After William disappears into the building, the reporter turns to face the camera and begins detailing what the pending case would have been. "Antonio Serrano was charged with first-degree murder for the death of twenty-one-year-old Shawn Gates over what was reported a drug deal gone bad. Mr. Serrano was said to have jumped over the fence of DA William Brandon's home just hours after being released on bail in an attempt to kidnap the only witness in the shooting. For safety reasons, her name hasn't been disclosed to the media, but she did suffer from some injuries during the attack at DA Brandon's home. We will bring more information when we have it. This is Ernesto Torres for NBC Dallas."

A wave of relief hits me that they didn't toss out my personal information, although they did give enough of William's information to make it easy to locate him. However, as a prosecutor, I'm sure many people who want to know where he lives will find him.

Taking another drink of my coffee, I see a commercial for *YOU* on Netflix and it reminds me that Crystal dropped off a Kindle for me, and William left his card so I could buy whatever I wanted on it. I'm not allowed to use my personal stuff until he tells me it's okay, so he told me to buy as many books as my heart desires. He obviously doesn't know the extent of my reading addiction. Getting the device off the charger, I open it up and create a new account. This process takes forever, but if I want to read, it's got to be done. And I need to read. I've been reading since I was four years old and I'll do it until the day I die.

Scrolling through the latest on Amazon's top lists, and I see one that intrigues me. Okay, I see a lot that intrigues me, but this one is calling my name. I know it's going to be filthy, sexy, and yet still sweet. I click on the buy now and impatiently wait for it to download. When I open it, I dive right in. Two hours later and I've only made a dent in the book, but it's so good that I don't want to put it down even though I should probably eat. At least I took something out for dinner.

My phone rings, so I'm forced to close the book, but seeing it's William, I pick up instantly. Talking to him on the phone is almost as hot as when he's in front of me. His perfectly even voice picks up as I tease him with lusty requests. It's all I can do to stop my racing heart as he tells me we're getting married. I should argue with him, but it's pointless. I want to marry the man more than anything in the world, so putting up a fight seems futile.

I fell in love with him by the end of our second day together, and he makes me want the happily ever after I only read about. The man makes my mouth water as he tells me about his hard cock. Immediately, a hand goes to my pussy, testing the little excited nub and my soaked panties.

By the time I hang up, I'm so soaked that I need a shower. What I really need is him between my legs, sending me soaring with orgasm after orgasm. It's funny how I spent all this time a virgin and the first time he makes me come, I become addicted. I suppose that's what drug addicts feel. I'm addicted to Beast. It's the most intense feeling in the world.

After showering, I toss on a pair of light ass-hugging shorts and a t-shirt. I'm not planning to go outside, but as much as I hate wearing a bra, I feel so uncomfortable without one. Maybe it's because my breasts are so large for my size. Once I'm good, I hop back in my position on the sofa with my tablet. When I finally finish this tasty morsel, I get up to start dinner. I know that William will be home soon, or at least that's what he said. I know his schedule can change depending on the work they need to do.

Chapter Thirteen

Beast

"I'm sorry, Mary. I'm on my way now." I turn onto the main highway from my office to Steeleville.

"It's okay. I know that you have a lot of work to do." The sound of her voice says she's not pleased at all. I can't say I blame her.

"You don't sound okay."

"I made dinner, but it's cold now," she confesses. I should have called her telling her I'd be late, but I knew that if I spoke to her, I'd push off work for another day.

"I'm sorry. I'm sure it'll taste great." She gives me a "humph," and I know I'm in deep shit.

"I'll be there soon." I end the call and hurry the fuck up. I have to get home to her and make it right. The sun starts to set even earlier, so it's pitch black on this road. Suddenly, I see a pair of headlights behind me, making me wonder. I start to slow down when they make an abrupt turn onto a dirt road that leads nowhere. The vehicle turns on the road and then starts going in the other direction and out of my sight. It's probably nothing. I nearly pull a U-turn myself and follow, but it's probably someone who made a wrong turn and is lost.

I'll tell the guys later at our meeting. I can't do shit about it now because I've got no information on the actual vehicle.

When I finally get into Steeleville, I feel a sense of relief. All I want to do is get to Mary, take her long and hard, and then repeat. Once I enter my gate, I point to the guards and tell them to go home. I don't want anyone around while I spend the rest of the night making up for being late.

I walk into the house, expecting to be reamed, but instead, Mary jumps into my arms, kissing me wildly. "Damn, babe. I missed you too." I carry her ass to our bedroom and strip her bare.

"I love you, William."

"I love you, Mary."

"Fuck me." She pulls on my suit jacket, sliding it off while I take off my tie.

"Hands." She moves to her knees and sticks out her hands. I wrap my tie around her wrists, leaving a long end for me to hold onto. "Sweet felony, you are being punished for what you did earlier today."

"What did I do?" She plays innocent, but she's got a sexy, devious smile on her face.

"You know damn well what you did. Getting me hard up at work, knowing that I couldn't put my hands on you until I got home." I drag her up to me by the tie and plant my lips on hers, thrusting my tongue into her mouth. I growl and then pull back. She sits on her feet while I stand and remove my clothes. My cock's stone solid and ready to fuck her pretty slender throat. I watch as she licks her lips, and as much as I want to punish her, I want to give her what she needs. I sit on the bed and then tug on the tie, bringing her head close to my throbbing dick. "Suck." The demand is low, guttural, and firm.

With her tied hands, she strokes my shaft from root to tip. I groan, feeling like I'm the one being pleasantly tortured. "Suck," I order, slapping my hand to her round ass that she's popped up for my viewing pleasure. A soft gasp followed by a moan escapes her lips, releasing a bit of heated air against my pre-come soaked head. Her tongue dips out, swiping all the liquid from the crown before she slides her hot mouth around me. With my hand massaging her ass, I press my middle finger over her little pucker, causing her to hum on my rod. "Fuck. You're going to make me come with that wicked little mouth of yours." I pull her off and bring her up for a kiss.

With her lips hovering over mine, she moans out, "You act as if it's a crime."

"It is when I'm trying to put my baby inside of you." Hooking my arm around her waist, I lift her to the center of the bed. "You're really a beast, carrying me with one arm." I take her tied hands and lift over her head. With one hand, I pump two fingers into her hot pussy. The sound of her juices coating my fingers drives me wild. I pull them out and suck off all her honeyed treat.

"You have no idea," I growl, sliding them back inside and then repeat licking them clean. "You're out of luck. I'm too damn hard up to wait for more than one orgasm out of your sweet cunt. You're going to get fucked hard and fast, and you're going to come when I say." I rub my thumb over her slit as I line up my cock, watching her body rock and hear her moans. Sliding into her heat, I lean down and suck her tit into my mouth, dragging my teeth over her tender flesh before moving to the other hardened nipple and feasting on her spectacular rack. Pulling off and out of her, I flip her onto her belly and cup her hips, dragging her ass up in the air.

Dipping my finger into her soaked core, I run it backward and rub it over her ass. "One day, I'm going to take this, and you're going to let me, right?"

"Yes…yeesss," she stammers, popping her ass back. I can't help myself, and I work my finger into her ass before, pumping my cock back into her tight pussy. She shudders and comes, squeezing both holes, gripping me so damn intensely, I nut deep into her womb, drenching her walls with jets of come. I pull out and plop onto the bed, dragging her on top of me.

"I hope I didn't freak you out. I don't know what came over me."

"I don't know, but I liked it. I want you to take me however you want." She brings her tied hands down over my jaw.

"Once I'm carrying your baby, I want to suck your come out of your cock, swallowing, letting it dribble down my chin, or letting you spray my body with it, so everyone knows I'm yours."

I lift her up on my still hard cock and slide her down my shaft. "Ride now. Work my come out, sweet felony. You got it stiff; you fix it." She bounces as I undo the tie. We fuck until we're both shouting the house down and her pussy is so damn full, my seed is dripping out. She falls forward, dozing on my chest.

I don't know how long we're there, but a notification hits my phone. It's still in my pants pocket, so I can't see who it's from. Then I remember that we have to be at the clubhouse soon. Laying with her in my arms is the best fucking feeling in the world, but I have a meeting tonight. I forgot to mention it to her.

I gently tap her shoulder. "Mary, don't fall asleep. The guys and I need to have a church session."

"Church? It's late." She looks over to the alarm clock, and it's nine-thirty.

"Not that kind of church. It's the kind we bikers have. It's our own personal meeting."

"Oh. How long will you be gone?"

"We'll be out for as long as it takes, but the women will be there to keep you company."

"Wait. You want me to come?"

"Of course I do. I told you the only reason I didn't want you around them before is that I couldn't outright claim you in public. Shit, part of me is glad Serrano did what he did, or I would have had to wait until January."

"I don't think I could have waited that long."

"Damn right. Me either. Come on. Let's get dressed and go."

"I need to shower."

"No the fuck you don't."

"Why? We don't have time, or do you want everyone to know that you've just fucked me to sleep?"

"Well, we do have some more time. How about we add an extra layer of hot, sweaty sex to your scent?" I growl, spinning so I'm on top of her. My cock grinds against her slit causing her to moan. My body comes alive with that sound. I drop my head and snake my tongue around her fat nipples licking them and then sucking each one until she's as riled up as I am.

"God! Fuck me, William. I need your cock."

"Good because that's what you're going to get." I line my tip up against her entrance and thrust home into her heat. Her tight warmth is my weakness. Everything about her is my weakness. I live for this woman from now until the day I die.

"Mary," I moan her name right before taking her mouth with mine, dipping my tongue inside, dueling with hers. I love the way she clings to me. Her hands digging into my sweaty back, marking her territory.

"I'm coming, William. Oh shit, I'm coming." Her legs flex as she cries out, sending me over the edge and coming deep in her. We kiss with a growling frenzied passion so intense that I nearly blackout from it.

"I guess it's time to get up now." I hate that we have

to leave, but it's important and most important to the two of us. The Riders are there for me.

I pull out and look at my still half-hard cock, wondering if it'll ever go down completely. I take my gaze off it and slide my eyes over to her. She's naked from head to toe. Glistening between her thighs is the remnants of us and like a beast, I don't want her to ever wash off my scent. I need to clean up a little and get dressed. I'll be ready in twenty minutes.

We enter the clubhouse, Mary's on my arm like the sexy candy she is, and the place is full except for Boomer and Crystal.

"Hey, Beast! You finally made it. Boomer's running late. He's busy drilling his wife."

"It seems like you were doing the same thing," Cyber adds. "And you must be Mary."

"I am."

"This jackass is Cyber."

"Well, he's not wrong." I love the way she doesn't hide our loving. It's one thing for me to be proud to nail her, but she doesn't have the shame, and it's hot as fuck.

"The rest of you, this is my woman Mary."

"Yeah, we saw on the news. I'm Wrench, and this is Cowboy and he's Rico."

Chapter Fourteen

Mary

"Can I get you a drink?" Roxie says. She's the only one I actually know. I haven't been introduced to the rest of the women here. She hands me a Mike's Hard Lemonade and takes my hand. "Boys, we'll be in the other room waiting for Crystal."

William comes up to me in his sexy vest and black tee, looking possessive as fuck. He pulls me away from Roxie and slams his mouth on mine for everyone to see. "Have fun, baby." He kisses my forehead and then walks back to the guys.

She hooks my arm and then leads me over to the other women. "Hi, Mary, I'm Sammie. You met my brother Doc already."

"And I'm Morgan. My husband is in the boys' room, but you already know both of my brothers Jackson and Boomer." So she's the one who decorated William's house. She's too sexy for me to believe nothing happened between her and my man, sending pure jealousy through me.

"I'm Penny. I saw you in the bar the other day." She blushes at the memory and my knowing smile. She must have had a lot of fun with the other Steele brother.

"It's a pleasure to meet all of you. I didn't know if he'd ever bring me around."

Morgan stands up and throws her arm over my shoulder. "These men can be protective and super jealous. Trust me when I say that he's just as bad as the rest. He didn't even trust his brother's not to hit on you." The ladies laugh, and Crystal walks in. She's flush and glowing with her growing belly.

"Hey, what's so funny?"

"We're just laughing at how bad Beast was the other night."

"Oh, my goodness. Your man has got it bad. Every time someone asked about you, he took another drink, grumbling that January was too far away."

"And then when I accidentally got him with the spray, he was scared you'd get the wrong impression," Morgan says. "He tried to bolt out of here without a ride home."

"I totally did get the wrong idea. It's so bad how pathetic I was. It's the reason I tried to leave."

"Girl, please. There isn't one of us that wouldn't flip out if our man came home smelling like another bitch," Crystal says, patting my hand.

"Yeah, but we weren't together."

"It didn't seem that either of you thought otherwise, but hey, it's where you two are now."

William walks in and straight to me. "Hey, babe, is everything okay?"

"Yes, why?"

"I'm just checking before we lock ourselves away."

"She's fine. Get going before Boomer drags you out by your ear," Morgan adds, slapping his hand away. He crushes his mouth on mine and then pulls back and leaves.

"He's got it bad."

"It's amazing, isn't it," I sigh.

"Looks like she's not any better," Roxie scoffs.

Crystal giggles and pulls out a bottle of water from the fridge. "Lost cause. Now when Roxie finds a guy with enough mettle, then we'll remind her how snobby she was to us."

"She's just jealous," I tease.

"Damn right. I need to find someone that makes me fucking fluffy and giddy as you broads."

There's a brief silence as the women eye Roxie, wondering where the softness came from.

Needing to take the heat off my friend, I ask, "So what do you do while you wait for them?"

"It depends. Mostly bullshit until they come back for us."

"Do you usually come with your brothers?" I ask both Sammie and Roxie.

"Not all the time if we're working, but they can be just as bad as the other guys and worry about our safety. It's crazy how we had no trouble until recently."

"Yeah, as soon as I came into town," Crystal says.

"No, you know that's not true. It started on the night

we met, and those fuckers were there for me," Morgan adds.

"So it's been a few months, and most of our lives have changed so much."

"Speaking of, how's Mick?" Sammie asks Morgan. A sad look comes over her face.

"He's improving, but you know it's a long process. Mostly he seems like he's back to normal, but I can tell he's hurting more than he's letting on." She seems so heartbroken.

"What happened to him?"

"It's almost two months now, but we were attacked, and they shot Mick and tried to kidnap Morgan." I shouldn't have asked. Now I feel even worse when her eyes begin to water.

"Oh, my goodness. I'm sorry."

She sniffles and takes a tissue from Crystal. "It's okay. My brothers and the rest of the guys made sure they paid for it." Just then, as if he knew she was upset, a tall, slightly thinner tatted guy comes in and grabs Morgan.

"My princess, why are you crying?" His Irish accent makes his words all the sweeter.

"Oh, nothing. You know how I've been."

"I've got to talk to the guys, so don't keep that shit up. I love you, and no one can take me away from you." He kisses her like it's his last, and I let out an audible sigh. He smiles up at me and says, "It's a pleasure to meet you, Mary." Then he leaves the room.

"Damn, that man. I've loved him for so long." She smiles to herself and sits down on a large microfiber sofa that screams comfort.

"He's handsome."

"Don't let Beast hear you say it."

"They're all handsome," Crystal says. "But I only have eyes for my man."

We all cheer to that. "Damn right."

"Hell yeah."

I'm really going to love these women.

Chapter Fifteen

Beast

"Okay, we're calling this meeting because Beast's incident is another reminder that the cartel is still going to be a big motherfucking problem we need to deal with. They have no intention of letting up on us, so we're going to strike when we can. I know most of you can't get your hands dirty and that's fine, but I need these people destroyed. They aren't coming into my town to dictate what happens here. They can keep their drugs and shove them up their coked out asses. I know you're working on getting some of them locked away, but it's never going to be enough. They want to grow their territory wherever they can. There are many rumors flying around about their activities in neighboring towns. I'm not everyone's savior, so they need their people to worry about that, but it's Steeleville that demands protection from all of you. Are you with me?"

A round of cheers and "fuck yeahs" go around the

room. "We need to get these fuckers and lay them out permanently. They have been a thorn in our side, and we can't have that, especially with our expanding families and businesses."

"I want you to dig into Serrano's records."

"I'm going to be doing that myself and hunting down Spencer for more information."

"Do you think he had something to do with it?" Wrench asks. "It's not like we haven't had our fair share of double-crossers."

"No, I don't think he's dirty. Besides, if that was the case, he would have waited until he had Mary in his custody. The DA believes the unsecured line Mary called Spencer on did the trick. Someone was listening in to his calls. I only used my secured lines to call him and made it vague. It's just a shitty lucky coincidence."

"Well, I'd keep my eyes open anyhow. None of these fuckers can be trusted. Too many of them are being dragged under the cartel's thumb. We're going to have a war. Knowing our allies is key. You can never be too sure with these outsiders," Law warns us.

"Have you busted any of these drug dealers lately?"

"No, but I have picked up a couple of druggies outside of town looking for a ride. They were fucking wasted at nine in the morning. I held them in lockup until they were picking at sores, and I had enough looking at their disgusting faces. I sent them over to a rehab place. I'm sure it won't work, but it was that or jail, so they went with the first option."

Cowboy shakes his head and scoffs, "You're good. At this point, I feel like popping these fuckers like they're fucking zombies on the Walking Dead." He lost his parents to a crackhead with a gun a long time ago. His sympathy for these people is zero and none of us can blame the guy.

"Okay, Daryl," Cyber says.

"I do have a nice crossbow," Cowboy teases. "Seriously, I feel like these geeked out fools are going to fuck with my cattle."

"Fuck, it's like some Dawn of the Dead type shit."

"You're not going to hoist them up in your barn and skin them, are you?"

"Fuck no. Who knows what diseases they've got. I don't want anyone, including my animals, infected."

"No joke. We don't want our residents hooked. All it takes is one hit to turn some of the best people into addicts."

"I need a beer," Cowboy grumbles, standing up out of his chair.

"Bring a round of beers in. We're not done," Boomer adds. Cowboy goes out to grab a bucket. It's nice to have a well-stocked bar in this place. He comes back a minute later and passes the bottles out. After tapping bottles, we toss them back before getting back down to business.

"I want their organization down on its knees. I want everyone to know we aren't to be messed with either."

"Of course we all want them dead, and at this point, I'm not above putting a bullet in each one of their heads," I add. Pulling that trigger had been as easy as breathing. I'd destroy anything or anyone who came after my woman. War was a part of my past and now is back in my present. This time, I have rules to play by, but then again, Steeleville's laws are a little lax when it comes to retribution. We went back and dug up some laws from the days of the Wild West and activated them. Stand your ground is the modern version of the rules, but we could push it if charged as long as we dropped the bodies in our town.

"What's the game plan? Are we going to sit back and wait, or lure those bastards into our backyards?"

"It's too dangerous to lure them here. We have our women and babies to consider. My wife isn't going to be getting shot because we brought the fuckers here, but if they show up, I will bury all those I can."

"Beast, I want you to start watching those around you at work. There's always someone in the pocket in law enforcement."

"Not that we would know anything about that," Law jokes.

"Understood. You've got me wondering if my office is bugged. Cyber, can you come in tomorrow and sweep it?"

"Absolutely."

Someone may have been listening and that's not cool for a multitude of reasons, but as an attorney, secrecy is a must. We continue to talk for another half an hour when Boomer's phone blows up.

"Uh, oh. We've left the girls too long," Jackson says.

"Yeah, Morgan says Crystal's fallen asleep. It's time to call it a night, brothers." We all shake up and walk out.

My eyes scan the room for my woman. She stands

up with a wide grin that makes my heart fucking jump. Wagging my finger at her, she comes to me, causing my cock to harden instantly. "I missed you, baby." I drop my head and steal a brief kiss on her soft lips.

"I did too," she sighs, hugging me.

"Did you have fun?" I ask, walking toward the door.

"Yes. The girls are hilariously entertaining," she says, smiling up as we walk to my truck. I help her inside and put on her seatbelt.

Leaning in, I kiss her cheek and add, "Crazy is more like it, but you didn't hear that from me."

She parts her lips and gasps, "I'm telling."

"I'm going to spank you," I growl, sliding my hand over her thigh and between her legs.

"Ooh, then I'm definitely telling," she stammers.

My thumb massages her slit as my mouth hovers over her neck, skimming my lips on her heated flesh. "You love being my bad girl, don't you?"

"Yes, William."

"Damn it, woman. I don't know how I'm supposed to drive with my dick so hard." I step back and close the door, walking around the front end to my side. Once inside, I open my pants to let my cock breathe. Her eyes widen and her lips part. Immediately, all I can picture is pushing her head down and let her slobber on my shaft until we get home. I'm about to whip out my cock when I hear the gravel move around us and see a pair of headlights. Shit. I forgot we were still in the clubhouse parking lot. Shifting it into drive, I pull out of the lot.

Chapter Sixteen

Mary

I can't believe that I'm getting married today. It's too wild. I've never been this happy before. It's been over two months since we got together and almost two days before Christmas. We were going to marry weeks ago, but his trial schedule kicked in and one lasted longer than expected. Finally, he's on vacation for the winter holidays, so we're standing in the middle of the Vegas strip, getting ready to say I do.

Roxie smiles at me and asks, "Are you ready?"

"Of course. How do I look?" I do a quick spin around in my below-knee white dress.

"Freaking fabulous, and I'm so jealous. Beast is going to lose his mind."

"Oh please. I'm sure you're going to find someone amazing one day. I really hope William finds me pretty today."

"The man drools over you in a pair of sweats. He's

going to have a hard time making it through the ceremony. So let's do this."

"Hold on. I want to make sure my hair's perfect." My long black hair is pinned up in curls that I had done an hour ago, so I'm certain they are going to fall soon. "You know Beast is waiting for you. The man is usually quiet and patient, but he's not today, so let's get a move on."

We exit my personal suite after one more evaluation of my appearance. The room is full of guests with about half the Riders and their friends. Boomer and Crystal manage to make it, although they will be heading home after the ceremony because her family is coming for Christmas. "You are a vision. Are you ready to get hitched?" Boss says as he sticks out his arm to lead me to William.

"Only to William."

"Shit. I done forgot that was his name." I roll my eyes and giggle. The hall doors open into the wedding chapel, and there he is. I'm at a loss for words on how handsome he looks in his black tux. The man wears a suit every day.

The second my eyes land on his, I see how I look to him. William forgets that Boss is supposed to walk me down to him. Instead, he jolts from his spot, eating away the distance between us.

"Hey, this is my part." Boss claps his hands to his waist, giving Beast the space to move between us.

"Sorry, old man. I can't wait anymore." He scoops me in his arms and carries me to the altar. Everyone around us erupts in laughter, but my heart isn't laughing.

It's pounding out of control. I love this man. My brow arches and I whisper, "You can put me down."

"Oh yeah." He sets me on my feet and smooths down my dress. "God, you look so damn beautiful."

He leans in and kisses my cheek and then turns to the officiant who is just staring at us. "Okay, we're good to go," he tells the officiant, twirling his wrist in a hurry-up manner. The ceremony is over in a flash and I find myself bent over in an amazing kiss to rival anyone's wedding.

"I love you, Mrs. Brandon."

"I love you too, my husband." He growls and scoops me up, cradling me all the way down the aisle. The man is insane, but no one else seems to care as they clap and cheer.

We all head into the Granite hotel restaurant for our scheduled wedding lunch and are directed to our tables. We're twenty minutes into our meal when a well-dressed man with two men following closely behind approaches our table. "Hello, I am Emiliano Martín. I'm the owner of this hotel, and I'd like to congratulate the happy couple."

William shakes the man's hand and says, "Thank you, Mr. Martín." He pulls me closer as if the owner has any interest in me. In fact, I don't think he's interested in me at all. His eyes land on Roxie, but she refuses to look up from her plate. Strange. Was she attracted to him? He's handsome.

"I'll let you continue your meal. Again, congratulations."

Another hour passes, and as William requests the

bill, he learns that it's been comped by the owner and to consider it a wedding gift. "Wow. That's fucking amazingly cool," Cyber says.

"I want to know who he knows," William says. "I don't like free stuff as a DA."

"We aren't even in Texas, so it's okay, but I'll still check him out."

"Thanks."

We part ways with our guests to head to our suite. My darling new husband looks aggravated. "Are you okay?"

"Yeah. I just don't like good looking rich bastards anywhere near my gorgeous wife."

"Are you serious?"

"I think anyone else would consider the hotel owner wiping our tab as a pleasant surprise."

"Well, maybe…just maybe I'm too hard up to care at the moment. It's been a whole twenty-four hours since I've been deep inside of you, and most importantly, I haven't consummated our marriage yet." The elevator doors open and it's empty, so we enter and as soon as the door closes, Beast earns his name. Growling, he lifts me up and pins me to the wall of the elevator with his stiff cock digging into my stomach. Shit, is it possible to come during a short elevator ride? He grabs my ass, gripping it firmly as he rolls his hips. The door pings and we practically stumble out as he carries me to our room. My hands run over his shoulders. His cock nestles between our bodies, grinding on my core with every step he takes, causing me to shimmy against him. "Relax. Is your pretty pussy aching?"

"Yes, William. I need you inside of me."

I hear the door lock beep, and then he uses his elbow to push down the handle, opening it for us. As soon as the door closes behind us, he wastes no time in getting us to our California King bed. He stands up and slides off his suit jacket while I reach for his belt. I need him naked and claiming me. Two minutes of frantic tearing at each other's clothes, he's buried deep inside me. "I love you, my wife."

We devour each other until the sun comes up.

Chapter Seventeen

Beast

It's been a month since we married, and the weather has been total shit for the past week. We had snow, rain, and slush. So it's nothing new, but for some reason, the sound of rain takes me by surprise. I'm immediately worried about my wife. She's working at the bar because Roxie caught a cold and they need her. She got a ride from Wrench and one prospect is there as well, but maybe it's the weather, but I have a bad feeling. I call her cell and she doesn't answer.

"Sir, you're going to be late if you don't leave now," my assistant informs me. I look at my watch and he's right.

"Shit. Okay. I'm coming." I'm due to meet with Detective Spencer and an informant of his to get down to how Serrano learned my address and when Mary would be leaving the house.

I get down to my truck and onto the road within a

few minutes. My phone goes off just as I turn onto the ramp for Dallas. I see my girl come up on my screen. Clicking the display on the dash, I greet my wife. "Hello, sweet felony."

"Beast, I came to your office. They said you just left and to check the lot and maybe you'd be there."

"What? Baby, why are you there?" She's supposed to be in Steeleville. Fuck, the unsettled feeling I had ramps up to pure panic.

"I got a message saying you wanted me to come here." Her voice becomes a hushed whisper. Fuck. Someone's fucking with us. If they lay a hand on her, I'll kill everyone involved.

"Oh shit. Someone is staring at me. I'm scared." Her voice cracks and so does my heart.

"I'm on my way. Please go hide somewhere." The call ends. I try to call her again but goes to voicemail. What the fucking hell? At least one of the prospects should have been with her.

Seconds later, my phone goes off, and it's Cyber. "Blade and I have her. She's safe. I intercepted the message. We followed her and waited for the person to make a move. It's a scrawny man that Boomer's got pinned down. The pic coming to your phone now."

Fuck. I click the image on my phone and roar out, "It's my assistant. The little rat bastard."

"We got him."

He rushed me out for a meeting, and now I know why. "I'm on my way back."

"She's scared, but she's not hurt."

"Then why isn't she on the phone?" I bark out, feeling livid that they even allowed her to be stalked.

"Because we want to know what you want to do with him."

"The Clubhouse."

"Understood. Here's Mary."

"William, I'm okay. Sorry." She's out of breath. I'm going to fucking kick their asses for not telling me what was going on before she was in danger.

"Babe, are you really?"

"I don't know what's going on. The guys came out of nowhere, and I felt like I could breathe again."

"I'm on my way to the clubhouse. Take it easy for me, my sweet felony."

"Drive safe, my love." I do my best, but I speed all the way there.

The second I'm the clubhouse lot, I jump out of my truck and run straight to Mary. I scoop her up and spin in a circle as she wraps her legs around me. I don't give two fucks that it's pouring down on us as I crush my mouth onto hers. Mary's fingers fork into my hair, kissing me like it's the last time. Fuck it could have been.

"I need to get you out of the rain."

"I don't care. I'm always wet for you." I crack up laughing and set her on her feet. That's just what I needed. That's the woman I'm madly in love with.

"I love you, too." I have too many questions that can't wait, and I have a special guest to welcome to the club or maybe to one of Blade's quality knives.

When we enter the clubhouse, Boomer's there with a pair of plyers in his hands.

"What the fuck, Boomer? Why didn't anyone call me?" I roar, losing my temper.

"Chill the fuck out. We tried. Your phone was going straight to voicemail until she called you. We thought you sent us to voicemail. He could have been sending an interference single while he was still in range of you."

"Are you serious?" It could explain why I couldn't get through to Mary while I was at the office.

"We're completely serious. We were surprised when she got through to you."

"Shit. Check my briefcase. I bet there's something in there. He handed it to me before I left eagerly."

We were about to walk back to my truck when a loud blast sends us backward. My arms are tightly wrapped around Mary as we hit the ground. I can feel footsteps around us. I hear something, but my ears are ringing.

My head's spinning as I try to move. Mary's not in my arms anymore, and I'm starting to freak out. I can hear Mary moan, sobbing my name. "Baby, I'm here."

"Let's get you both inside," Blade says.

"Where's Mary?"

"I'm here." I turn my head that's pounding like hell to see my wife in Boomer's arms. We're in the clubhouse, and I reach out to my wife. I'm going to kill Francisco.

"I'm bleeding," Mary sobs.

"You're going to be okay."

"No, the baby." Shit. The baby? Tears well up in my eyes, and my heart starts to crack.

"Baby?"

"I'm sorry. I wanted to tell you today." She cries, and

I reach out, forgetting all about my pain and pull her to me.

"It's going to be okay, my love. I'm sorry about our little one." I kiss her temple, attempting to be brave for her.

The love of my life's carrying my baby, and we may have lost it. There's no way in hell this is going to happen legally. Thinking about what he had planned infuriates me to the core. I would be dead and unable to protect Mary for whatever they had in store. My guys foiled Francisco's plans and saved our lives.

"I'm sorry, brothers." If it wasn't for them, we wouldn't be here.

"No need to be sorry. You know we'd be the same way."

"Doc, they're over here."

He comes to us, but I wave him off. My wife needs to be the priority. "Take care of Mary first, please."

"I think both of you need to go to the hospital. The ambulance is already on the way. Don't argue with me."

"Don't worry about the other issue. We'll keep him waiting for you."

"Thanks." The sound of sirens can be heard even inside the clubhouse.

"Let me get them in here with the stretcher for Mary."

"It's already too late. I've lost the baby."

"We don't know that. It's possible to bleed and not lose the baby. Just do us all a favor and give Beast some relief and get treated properly."

"Thanks, Doc. Please, sweetheart."

"I will for you."

The ride to the hospital seems to take forever. Mary's lying on the stretcher with me and the medic on one side while Doc is on the other. "Ma'am," I'm going to put an IV in, okay?"

She nods, turning her head towards me.

"William needs to be treated as well."

"We will take care of him as soon as we arrive. Unfortunately, getting another ambulance out over here is hard. There are accidents all over the city." Suddenly, I feel lousy and drained, and things go black.

I wake up a few hours later, and Mary is lying in bed next to me asleep. "Ah, you're awake," Boss says.

"Hey, yeah. What's going on?" I choke out, feeling like I'm in the damn desert.

Boss grabs a cup of water with a straw and brings it to my lips. "Well, you almost died, and your pretty wife freaked out."

"What?" I spit the straw out.

He sets it down before patting my hand that's connected to a saline drip. "Yes, the bombing happened yesterday, and you were in surgery for three hours."

"You're kidding with me," I scoff, trying to get up and go to Mary. Immediately my body protests, and I fall back onto the pillow behind my head. There's a pain in my side.

"What about Mary? The baby?"

"I'm fine, my love and so is your little beast," she sighs. "You protected us." Relief flows through me. Fuck, I almost lost everything again. I need my Mary in my arms, but knowing she's going to be okay makes it better. And she's having my baby.

"I'll do everything in my power to protect you, my sweet felony. I love you."

Chapter Eighteen

Mary

IT'S BEEN WEEKS SINCE THE ATTEMPTED MURDER AND kidnapping, and I still have a hard time when William is away from me. I don't tell him that, though, because he needs to recover and not worry about my feelings. Morgan wraps me up in a hug when I enter the secure room at the clubhouse. Having been through this, she understands the fear I live with. "Thanks for keeping me company while they deal with that bastard that tried to kill us."

"No problem. We've all had moments like this because of the cartel. We're just glad that you and Beast are on the mend."

"Thanks, Morgan." She's not the only one here. All the women are gathered while the men talk shop and plan their confrontation with Francisco Soto. "So, what do you think they're going to do?"

Crystal walks up to me, gives me a quick hug, and then answers flatly, "Well, they'll kill him; that's for sure, but I'm betting they're going to do it slowly. This is weeks in the making. He's been held this entire time."

"Enough of the ghastly talk. How about we talk about our babies coming? I'm so happy that we can all share that." Sammie, who married Crystal's brother, is also pregnant, so we're all commiserating together. Crystal is the farthest along, but all of our babies will be growing up together. It's going to be so sweet.

"For all the babies he wants, we're going to need a much bigger house," I laugh out.

Crystal rubs her belly with a big smile. "I'm telling you. Shit, we're going to need a bigger town with all the kids these men want." I'm sure Boomer wants his name to carry on, so he's probably going to keep her knocked up for the foreseeable future.

"I know, right?" Sammie adds, rubbing her invisible bump.

"They are all too damn masculine," Crystal sighs, rolling her eyes.

"Are you complaining?" I ask, secretly loving that I got a beast of a man.

"God, no. I love my intense man. Who doesn't love a man that would move mountains because it would ruin your view? I mean these guys are so everything wonderful that you almost forget all the bad things that come along with being at the top," Crystal says. She's married to the town founder, making him a huge target for the drug world that's ripping through the United

States, so she knows better than all of us what lies ahead for her.

"Is anyone else starving?" Penny asks, rubbing her belly too.

"I need some food."

"How about we go somewhere to eat?" Penny suggests.

"Yeah, the guys aren't going to like that idea. Just because they have one guy doesn't mean that we're out of danger."

"I know, but maybe they could go get us some food instead," I suggest.

"Damn, why did you have to mention food? I could really go for some pancakes," Morgan grumbles.

"Let me ask." Crystal sends a message to Boomer.

Ten seconds later, her phone pings back. She reads it then lifts her head with a giddy smile. "My man is a wise one."

"What's up?" I ask.

"He said the food is on the way. He ordered it a while ago."

We're all cheering, which is terrible considering they are probably torturing him in the other room.

My phone rings, and it's William. "Hey, baby." His greeting automatically ruins my panties. The man's voice should be on commercials, in movies, or whatever, but then again, I refuse to share him with anyone.

"What's going on?"

"I've got to take a ride, so I'm going to be out of contact for a little bit. You'll be fine with everyone here."

His reassurance right now means absolute dick to me. After everything we've been through, I'm having serious panic attacks when we're apart.

"Um...is everything all right?" I choke out. Damn, I need to get my act together. *Breathe, girl. Don't cry.*

"Yeah. I just need to get going, though. I love you. I'll see you in a couple of hours."

"Hours?"

"Sorry, but yes. I love you, Mary."

"I love you, too." And my mood instantly soured. I don't know where he's going, but he didn't come to say goodbye to me.

"Girl, what's wrong?" Roxie asks, seeing that I'm fighting back the tears.

"He has to go somewhere and won't be back for a couple of hours." That's when the tears run down my cheeks.

"Oh, it's going to be fine." Morgan brushes off my worry, giving me another hug. "Trust the guys."

"I know, but he didn't do it in person." Even to myself, I sound pathetic, which only makes the tears come out more.

"He's probably covered in blood, sweetie," Crystal explains, rubbing my arm like it's commonplace for them to be covered in someone's blood.

"Yeah, he probably doesn't want to touch you when he's got that bastard's blood on his hands."

"I suppose." I let out a soft sob and then choke it back because I'm being ridiculous. Everything they are saying makes a lot of sense, so I try to change my mood.

Straightening my back, I ask, "Did Boomer say what he ordered?"

"Breakfast and lunch options. He said with so many pregnant women, options were a must."

"He really is a smart man," I say.

About ten minutes later, the men come into the secured portion of the clubhouse that's meant for when they want to keep us out of harm's way. The smell of meat hits my nose, and my stomach does somersaults. I'm on my feet to the bathroom as fast as I can.

Roxie, who helped bring in the food, comes in to check on me. "Shit, Mary are you cool?"

"Yeah, it's the whole pregnancy thing."

"Damn, I hope that doesn't last long."

"Thanks. You don't have to stay in here if you're going to be sick."

"Come on. Do you think I'm that weak? I'm worried about you. Your face paled, and then you took off. I'm just concerned."

"You're a wonderful friend."

"Thanks, but I'm sure the rest of them would be in here if they could manage to not get sick as well." I stand and move to the sink and get cleaned up.

The cool water on my face feels so good. "I'm going out there again."

"Are you sure that's a good idea?"

"I'm hungry, and I've got nothing left in my stomach, so I'll hold my nose and get some food." We go out, and everyone asks if I'm okay now. Funny that even though I can smell the meat this time, it doesn't send me into the bathroom again.

I scoop up some hash browns and bacon and move out to the main area to sit down. I turn the television on, and there's my husband on the news. I press the volume to hear what they're saying.

"DA Brandon, it's great to see you return to work again."

"Oh, I'm just here for a meeting or two, but then I have to get back to my wife."

"Do you know who attacked you?"

"I don't, but I have my suspicions. Once I find out, there will be hell to pay."

"You know that little scar on your eyebrow adds another sexy element to your persona. The ladies are probably loving this segment."

"Well, the only lady I care about is my wife. She's the one whose opinion matters to me."

"Rumors are that it's your former assistant who fled the day you nearly died."

"I can't say exactly. I'd hate to think that someone that close to me did this, but at this point, it can't be ruled out. Now, if you'll excuse me, I need to make the most of the time I have while I'm at the office."

"Thanks again for your time, DA Brandon." Will heads into his building, and then the same reporter who I saw last time turns to the camera to address his anchor in the studio.

"It's great to see DA William Brandon back to work after nearly being blown to bits a few weeks back. He's a determined man, and his wife must be a lucky woman."

The in-station anchor says, "You sound envious. I know I am. Congratulations to the newly married Mrs.

Brandon. You've got the cream of the crop." They go to commercial, and I'm betting it's because they're all flustered over my sexy husband.

"Damn, that man was trying to scam on your hubby. I'd fuck his ass up."

"That's hilarious. That woman in the studio is blushing."

"I'm going to kick her in the cunt in about a minute. Beast is lucky that bitch was in the studio not outside interviewing him, or I'd fuck them both up."

"Ah come on, he's just doing his job," Jackson says, taking a seat on the sofa next to me.

I roll my eyes at him and nod. "I'll remind you of that the next time a man comes into Penny's bakery and flirts with her."

Suddenly his expression changed, and he throws his hands up. "Okay. You got me there."

"Damn right. Excuse me, I need some more food," I say, getting up to head into the kitchen.

"Shit, working in a bar got her a little feisty," Cyber says, having watched us talking shit.

"Or she just loves her man and almost lost him twice, so fuck off, Cyber." Roxie follows behind me, making me laugh.

"Wow, do you and Cyber have a thing going on?"

"Hell no. He's a nosy ass." She stares at the door as if Cyber can feel her anger from the other side.

"Uh oh, did he like scope out your browsing history or something?"

"Something like that, but I don't want to talk about it." Whoa someone is a little more than testy.

"You know, you and I are super close. You can tell me anything. I won't tell anyone."

"Yeah, I know."

I can see that she doesn't want to talk, so I let her be. "Okay. I'll give you some time alone."

Chapter Nineteen

Beast

"It's been weeks since I saw my assistant. I say it's time to rectify that," I state, giving Blade a knowing look. I've already decided what I'm doing with him. The guys left him in the room without harming the little fuck because they wanted my say in the matter. He's on the run from the law on suspicion of attempted murder, so no one is aware we swiped the fucker. After the bomb had been placed in my briefcase, it was easy to figure out who did it.

Boomer opens the door, and sitting in the corner is the squirrely bastard. "You tried to kill me. You tried to kill my wife. You almost killed my baby. Now, what should I do about it?"

"You've been starving me for weeks."

"Now you know that's not quite true. You've been given food. Not that you deserve it. You've lived three weeks longer than you should have. I should have strung you up by your balls that same day, but I didn't understand the depths of your depravity."

"Wait. Listen. I can give you information on the others."

"My brothers have informed me about your activities. You gave up your cards last week." I step closer to him, watching his face contort.

"Not all of them?" He shakes as I continue to approach.

"Oh, really. What makes you think I'm gonna believe anything you have to say now?"

"Because he's been betraying you this whole time." A smirk on his face sends my fist into his gut.

I grab his head and jerk his head back. "Who?"

"Spencer."

"Yeah?" A knot in my stomach forms, but I'm not that gullible. He better have some evidence to back that shit up.

"He sold out to the cartel last year to drugs and money. He's the one who brought Serrano to your house."

"Bullshit." I can't imagine being that fucking double-crossed.

"You don't believe me?"

"Not. At. Fucking. All." Even as I say it, I wonder if it's possible.

"Don't you people have cameras? How do you think he got there so fast after the call without knowing where you live? It's not like the land is marked well or on fucking Google Maps."

"Francisco, if you're lying to me, I'm going to take

pleasure in torturing you until your heart can't handle the blood loss, and you die. If you are telling the truth, I'll give you a fighting chance for survival."

I watch as a glimmer of hope crosses his face, which sends another wave of doubt washing over me. Fuck, I can't believe Spencer's behind it. I step out of the room, leaving him with two guards while I go into the security room to check his accusation. "Cyber, bring up the furthest camera from my house from the day of the attack on Mary." It's the camera on the outskirts of Steeleville.

"Why? Is there something we missed?"

"Maybe."

"It would have taken Serrano about ten minutes to get to my house from where we saw him on the other cameras. Now, if he planned to take her away and make her disappear, he'd have to have a getaway car, but we didn't see one. I can't believe I fucking missed it."

"What do you mean?"

"Who's the only car you see before any of the Riders show?"

"Detective Spencer's car," he says, but we all believed he was there to pick up Mary like she asked.

"Let's look at the edge of town." He cues up the footage. He hits play, I'm fucking instantly sick to my stomach. There's Spencer's car parked on the outskirts as Serrano walks away from it. Ten minutes later, Spencer's car begins to move slowly through Steeleville to my home by the time Serrano should have kidnapped Mary, but he failed and was bleeding out, so Spencer came to my gate pretending to be innocently arriving at Mary's request.

"Fuck. I'm sorry, bro. Maybe we're mistaken."

"No. There's no mistaking that betrayal. Flash drive that shit. We're not going to kill him. The most fucked up place for a cop isn't hell—it's prison." I crack my knuckles. "Excuse me while I deal with the other piece of shit."

"Of course." I go back into where we were keeping Francisco. "Did Spencer set up that meeting with me for you to ambush Mary and blow me up?"

"Yes, of course. He threatened to kill my sister if I didn't," he insists, but I'm betting it's more to do with the scratching he's been doing since he got here. He's not a full-blown junkie, but he was on his way. I wouldn't have known if it wasn't for his attack on Mary and his subsequent scratching.

"Oh, really? And you couldn't get help instead of attacking my family?"

"Spencer's my ex-brother-in-law."

"Wow, things are getting more interesting by the minute. You must really want to live." I wrap his head in a black hood, then drag his ass out to the SUVs and stuff him in the back of one. It's already dark out when my plan starts to take shape. I've no intention of letting him live and the more I think about Spencer the less I care if he suffers. I want him dead.

The middle of the night can be freezing this time of year in the middle of the Arizona desert.

The next morning, Spencer enters my office, and I play the game according to plan. Shaking his hand and offering him a cup of coffee. "I'm sorry about the shit with your assistant. What the fuck was he thinking?"

"I don't know. He had to be working with Serrano or someone that hates me. I haven't found the fucker, but when I do, I've no idea what I'm going to do."

"I have men looking for him, but there are no signs of him anywhere." His phone rings, but he doesn't answer it, and I know why. It's the answer I need. It's the nail in his coffin.

"Will, I've got to go. I have a meeting with my partner. I just came to check in on you."

"Thanks. I'm glad to call you a friend. Let me know if you find my former assistant."

"I will."

We shake hands, and he leaves, looking back twice. A nervous expression passing across his face before quickly being masked. I go back to my office and send out some emails. For the next eight hours, I remain completely at work with limited contact with Mary. As long as the guys have her safe and I'm at work, we can't be tied to what's about to go down.

When it's time to leave, I go straight home where Boomer and Cyber are waiting.

"Hey, give me a minute. Where's my woman?"

"I'm right here," Mary hollers, running into the living room and into my arms. Damn, I feel blessed as I kiss her soft lips and taste strawberries. Growling, I grind my dick into her, forgetting we have an audience. Boomer's throat-clearing reminds us, and I set her on her feet.

"So, everything worked perfectly."

"Great." A buzz at my gate catches our attention and stops all talk. I look at the camera and it's a Dallas police vehicle. I press the intercom. "Can I help you officer?"

"Yes. I'm Detective Lewis and my partner Detective Greenlee. May we speak with you?"

"Come on through." I press the button, and the guys are prepared.

I look down at Mary and then kiss her lips. "Please go into the kitchen with the girls."

"Okay. Please be safe." I wink, and she walks away.

Boomer nods, giving the go-ahead, so I open the door to the detectives. "DA Brandon, thank you for seeing us." They step inside, spotting both of my guys.

"We didn't realize you had company." Suspicion strikes not only me, but it's written on my friends and brother's faces.

"It's fine. I have to have security around me at all times because of this bullshit."

"Well, that's good. We hate to say this, but we believe something happened to Detective Spencer."

"What do you mean *something happened* to Spencer?"

"He's missing," Lewis says.

"Missing? I saw him this morning at my office." It's true. Although I know he's not missing. He's in the middle of the desert with Francisco.

"Yes, that's why we are here. You were the last person known to have seen him." That's fair.

"Well, I don't know if I can be of any help. He left quickly. He said he had to meet with…who did he say again…give me a second to…ah yes. Spencer said he was meeting his partner, whoever that is." His last partner had been killed in a car accident wholly unrelated to being a cop, so I don't know who they added to replace him.

"What? That's me," Detective Greenlee states, looking completely surprised.

"He received a call on his phone that he let go to voicemail and then excused himself less than a minute later." Lewis makes a note, but Greenlee seems dismayed.

"He didn't talk to me all day," he exclaims, appearing guilty. If I didn't know the truth about Spencer, I'd wonder.

"I'm sorry, but that's what he said. I hoped he'd come to bring me good news about my former assistant. Unfortunately, he didn't and made his visit much shorter than usual."

"Damn. I hate to say it to you, DA Brandon, but we have to inform you that Detective Spencer may be a part of the attack on you and Ms. Stark." He's nervous, apparently reading the rage on my face. Even though I already knew that thinking about it easily infuriates me.

"What?" I jump up. "Spencer's my friend."

"Sorry, but we have found evidence that he and your assistant were once brothers-in-law."

I run my hands through my hair. "Son of a bitch. I

had no idea." I pace the room, clenching and unclenching my fists. Stopping, I ask, "Do you think he's helping Francisco hide?"

"I don't know. His phone records have been pulled, but all we know is he received a call that came from Francisco's phone. He should have informed us." I pretend to be surprised.

"I wonder…God, I hope he's not involved."

"Unfortunately, that's not something we believe. We hoped that he'd tell you more while he was with you."

"I'm sorry. I wish he did, but if I'd found out, I would have killed the bastard right there." I clench my fists in rage, wishing I could have gotten away with killing him myself.

"We tried to put a trace on his vehicle, but we couldn't get the warrant in time. He left your office too soon, and then we lost him in the Dallas freeway." Lewis grunts in frustration, nodding in agreement with Greenlee's words.

"Don't you have trackers on all of your vehicles?" Cyber asks.

"Yes, but today was his day off. He had his own vehicle," Lewis tells him.

"Damn. So what's your game plan? I'm probably going to need more security." I finish that last part almost to myself.

"Thanks for the vote of confidence," Boomer mutters.

I turn to my longtime friend and shrug. "Sorry, but I need to keep Mary protected at all times. I'm not going to let anyone endanger her."

"We can add our own police."

"Sorry, Detective Lewis, but that's a hell no. If I can't trust people close to me, there's no way I'll trust someone who probably worked with Spencer."

"I figured you'd say that."

"We'll do our best to find him. We're sorry," Greenlee adds.

"Thanks for driving out here to break the news to me." I huff out a sigh.

"No problem. If something happens to you, the media will be all over our ass. We don't want to deal with that. We'll be going. We have to find his ex-wife. She's missing as well."

"Really?" I'm completely baffled about that one. I hadn't even thought about her in this.

"Yes, but that bothers us even more. What if he's done something to her?"

"I don't know. I've never met her, but Spencer didn't seem to have anything negative to say about her the few times he mentioned her."

"Thanks again, DA Brandon." Greenlee stands, outstretching his hand. I shake it and then Lewis's hand. I walk them out and then come back inside.

When I come back in, Cyber waves a device. "I've already swept the area to see if they added a listening device. They didn't."

"Thanks."

"Everything is good. He reacted just as expected. Tomorrow's the shipment date for a load of heroin. Border Patrol received an anonymous tip."

"Oh, wonderful. Now, if you'll get out of my house so I can fuck my wife, that would be great."

"We'll have guys around the perimeter all night just to keep up appearances," Boomer says before marching into the kitchen. A minute later, a giggling Crystal is being carried out in his arms.

"Have a good night. I know we will," she squeals as they leave. Cyber smirks and then closes the door behind him. I double lock it and then look for my woman who's still in the kitchen.

"We're alone."

"I know, but dinner's almost done. So we'll eat, and then you can bend me over the table and fuck my brains out."

"How long do we have until it's done?"

"Ten minutes."

"Then we have plenty of time." I grab her around the waist, dragging her mouth to mine before spinning her around with her ass against my stiff dick. Skimming my hands down her arms and around her front, I unbutton her pants, dip my thumbs inside, and pull them off. She steps out of the rest. I lower my slacks down to my thighs, freeing my achingly hard cock. Nudging her panties to the side, I rub my tip against her folds, testing her need.

A little shiver of delight runs through her body, and then I take what's mine. Bending her over the kitchen island, I thrust my cock deep into her pussy in one long stroke. "Ahh," she moans, pushing her ass back to impale herself on my shaft. Reaching up, I lift off her blouse and grab her bra covered tits, holding onto them as I fuck her hard and fast.

"That's it, Mary. I want you to come around my cock."

"Fuck, William. So good." She squeezes her walls fiercely around my length as I pinch her nipples.

"I love taking you like this. Your round ass bouncing on my dick like you want it."

"I always want it. Give it to me." I pump harder, rocking the damn island and knocking over a bottle of water. Pressing my hand into the pool of water on the surface, I lean back and spank her pretty ass with my wet hand.

"I'm coming. Shit. Again, Beast. Spank me." I repeat it on the other ass cheek, emptying my own load of come into her. Breathless, I pull out of her pussy and adjust her panties to catch most of my come.

"Ooh, we still have three minutes."

"Well, in that case, let me clean up your cock." She grabs the water bottle, dribbling a little bit of the water on my shaft as she sucks on the tip.

"Good girl. You need to stay hydrated." I grip her hair, dragging my fingers along her scalp and lead her head down to my cock. Her cheeks hollow out as she continues to suck me off. I'm about to come again. Taking me as far as she can go, she strokes the rest of my shaft with her hand. "Shit, I'm about to give you a special drink."

"Good, I'm thirsty." On those words, I shoot my load. She swallows every drop before standing like she didn't just suck out my soul. Smiling, she adds, "Dinner's done."

"So am I." I'm boneless as I try to stand, leaning against the counter. I don't know what's come over her, but I love it.

Chapter Twenty

Beast

I exit the courtroom to a crowd of microphones, phones, and cameras. "DA Brandon, are you relieved that Francisco Soto is dead?"

"Can we get a comment?"

"What? Excuse me." I push past them because I don't even know what's going on. I've been in court since eight. Although I'm guessing they found the bodies this morning.

"DA Brandon." They continue to shout, but I don't have any patience for this. I whip out my phone and walk to my SUV. I have two Riders who wait for me to drive off before they jump in their pickup to follow behind.

"Call Sweet Felony." My Bluetooth in the car dials Mary because I need to hear from her before I go into the office.

"Hey, beautiful."

"I love you. Have you heard the news?"

"No."

"Francisco Soto is dead, and so is Detective Spencer. They killed each other according to speculation."

"Oh, wow. I knew he was shady." She doesn't know the extent of Spencer's involvement, but she's aware that he was helping Serrano.

"I feel so much better now. A tiny bit safer."

"I'm glad for that. At least something good comes from their deaths, but enough about them. I want to talk about you."

"I'm aching today in all the right places, and I want you to come home because I'm feeling really horny. I want your big dick down my throat while you fuck my face."

"Fuck, are you trying to make me crash?"

"Oh shit. You're driving?"

"Yeah. Sorry, I should have said that." My cock is like a steel rod right now. Luckily, I only have two more blocks. "I think you just enjoy getting me hard when I can't do anything about it."

"Are you going to punish me?"

"Damn right. I'm going to come down your throat, and then I'm going to spread you out and take my time dragging several orgasms from your pussy before I bury my cock deep in your ass."

"I'll be ready when you get home. I love you." She ends the call with a giggle. I love that she's constantly giddy and horny. Damn. I love her pregnant. I'm going to have to keep her that way.

When I get into my parking spot, I see a crowd of

reporters waiting for me. Adjusting my dick, I jump out of my new SUV and grab my leather messenger bag.

"Can we get a comment, DA Brandon?"

I stop and clear my throat. "My wife just informed me of the deaths after seeing it on TV. Sorry. I'm still processing the news. It's sad to lose a friend. However, the one responsible for the attack on my wife and myself won't be around to try again, so I'm grateful for that. Now, if you'll excuse me, I still have a lot of work to do." I enter the building and to my office suite.

It takes about two hours before Erica buzzes my phone. "Yes?" I ask.

"Sorry, sir. DA Madden is here along with two detectives to see you."

"Okay. Send them in."

I stand and greet them as they walk in. "DA Madden, Detectives Greenlee, Lewis. I've just heard the news."

"Yes. Unfortunately, we've learned some disturbing information about Spencer's behavior. After examining his home last night, we found his ex-wife. She's in the hospital after being held captive by Spencer. Apparently, he was still obsessed with her."

"I hope she's going to make it."

"Yes, most of her wounds are superficial. A lot of bruising, but I'm sure the emotional wounds are going to take the longest to heal."

"So, what actually happened?"

"You know the call he sent to voicemail came from Francisco Soto. A string of texts shows that he was asking for help to get out of the country and drugs. He was losing it. He'd been hiding out in abandoned buildings and in a drug house."

"Wow. I had no idea he used drugs. He used to be skittish around me, and it drove me nuts, but I can't believe he had a drug problem."

"It's unfortunate. Some of the best people can fall into that trap with one dumb decision. We'd like to say the threat is over for you and your wife, but we also learned that Spencer had ties to the cartels. Nothing concrete, but we have our suspicions."

"I'm trying to process all of this. Just a few months ago, I was singing Spencer's praises for bringing my wife to me. Now I learn I'd been his mark the whole time."

"We're sorry. We have a lot to go over with the media."

"Again. We're truly sorry." They walk out while I get back to work. I'm trying not to think about how I'd been betrayed, but despite the fact that they're both dead, their actions still fuck with my sense of well-being.

A minute later, a message shoots to my phone. It's from Mary. ***My pussy aches for you. Come home soon. Dinner will be late tonight.***

Working hard, I clear my desk and leave ten minutes earlier than expected. I need my wife naked and coming on my dick.

I'm almost to the house when Cyber calls. "Line's clear. Can you stop into the clubhouse? There's something we want you to see."

Damn it. I drive to the clubhouse and meet with the whole crew.

"We set up a special listening device just outside

their meeting area in the middle of the desert that we didn't let the cops get ahold of." Everything worked according to plan.

They cue it up.

"You came to the wrong person Francisco. I can't have you telling everyone my involvement with Cortes." Spencer's voice is filled with vitriol and crazy. The man was a total psychopath.

"I swear. I...I...I...never said anything."

"But you can if they get their hands on you, and everyone is looking for you."

"I'm not going to let you."

"Whoa. Where did you get that gun?"

"I stole it." A newfound confidence can be heard in Francisco's voice.

"Are you working for the cartel now?"

"Maybe I am. Maybe they're watching."

"So you made me come out here so that you could kill me? Is this your way in? You fucking loser addict! If you kill me, your sister is dead. No one knows where she is."

"She can handle herself." I can't tell who fired first, but the sound of two gunshots go off and loud thumps, which is probably the bodies hitting the ground. I can hear sounds of sand moving, and I'm guessing it's the sound of one of them crawling.

"Well, I guess Francisco didn't underestimate, Spencer."

"We knew that Spencer had no intention of letting him live, but Soto thought if he played ball that he could run as soon as Spencer was arrested."

"Yeah, he wouldn't have lasted another day out in the desert if he didn't follow our requests." We set the meeting up and brought Francisco with the help of some less than reputable friends.

"The policed tied the gun to Shawn Gates."

"It must have been what they were looking for in his room or at least a bonus weapon. His parents didn't know he owned one from what Law learned while sniffing around today."

"A stolen gun could come in handy when trying to commit murders." Damn, I wish the bastard was still alive, so I could kill him myself.

I had so much rage built up from every single thing they had put my little family through. I'll never be able to let that concern disappear. Mary and our baby are my life and I'd do anything to keep them safe. Anything.

Epilogue

Beast

I RUB MY BABY'S SOFT HEAD, KISSING THE FUZZ AS HIS mommy rests on our bed. It's been two days since Will was born. I never thought that I would have a son and that I'd name him after me, but Mary made me fall in love with my own name, especially when it comes from her lips. She's the most enchanting woman in the world. "Come on, son. We have some documents to go over, and I'm going to need to train you as my new assistant."

He looks up at me with sleepy eyes not understanding a word I'm saying. "Fine, I'll give you the day off, but I expect you to start shaping up, mister." I carry him down to my office where his bassinet is and set him inside while I work. Mary needs all the sleep she can get after bringing this little guy into our lives after twenty hours of labor. I started to worry that they'd have to cut him out, but apparently, not all women were like Crystal having the baby on the side of the road.

Once he's settled, I get to work on my latest venture. We're still after the cartel, but like any criminal organization, taking out the leader only gives way for a new man in charge. It's been the wildest nine months of my life and I wouldn't change it for anything.

I work for what feels like minutes, but by the sun setting, I'd say at least three hours have passed. The sun doesn't set until eight at night during these scorching Texas summers, but it's been a wonderful day. The movement in the bassinet tells me that I better start taking him to mommy for some food and see if she'd like a late dinner. With three new restaurants in the area, we have more options for takeout which helps with this one.

"Come on. Are we ready to see momma?" He doesn't answer me, which I find rude and I tell him. "You know? Am I going to have these one-sided conversations for a long time or what?"

"I'm guessing at least a year."

"Babe, what are you doing out of bed?"

"My boobs started to hurt, so I came in here to see if he was hungry."

"I'm sorry. We were just about to go get you."

"Let's get you situated."

"How about in the living room? I'm starting to feel a little claustrophobic in the bed most of the time."

"Funny, I don't recall you being claustrophobic while we were making him."

"Yep. Well, I have to stay still. With you, I got a full workout and needed to lay down."

I grab pillows from one side of the sofa to help prop

her up in a comfortable position. Breastfeeding is no easy task. "I'll bring your water jug." She has a mini, keg-like water bottle that she has to drink while feeding the baby to stay hydrated. I pick it up and fill it a little more than halfway. As I come back into the room, I see my boy working hard to get his fill. He's growing fast. Two days and I swear he feels heavier.

"Do you need anything else?"

"Just you. Unless you're busy or uncomfortable."

"Never when it comes to you. Only a little envious," he says, swiping his tongue over his lips.

"Dirty old man."

"Damn right. Now let me hold you both." I wrap my arms around my family while Mary cradles our son to her chest. We both relax together. It's a perfect moment that I hope stays that way. Life has been too hectic for so long that it's nice to go a day without any drama. Well, I suppose with a baby it's a new set of dramas and a hectic lifestyle.

I love my family and can't wait to add to it. Five weeks and five days to go.

A year later

Mary

Six months pregnant with baby number two is no different than the first. I'm so horny that I can't wait for William to get home from work. I look at the clock several times, and it's frustrating. It's only twelve. He's in court all day. "Ugh." I plop myself onto the sofa.

Our baby is napping in his room, so I bust out my tablet and open up a favorite re-read Mine by Elena M. Reyes. Being the wife of a DA, I shouldn't be reading about antiheroes, but I love Thiago and his wicked ways. Shit, I'm overheated, and I haven't even started reading.

Three hours later, I've finished the book, and now I'm more bothered than I was this morning. Luckily the baby helps keep my mind off of sex. He's happily playing on the floor on one of his awesome playmats that I got from Roxie on his birthday. I love my son and my other boy who's on his way.

My phone rings on the coffee table, echoing too

A year later

loudly, scaring the baby. He cries as I answer it. "Hey, baby. Is everything okay?"

"Yeah, the phone startled him."

"I'm sorry, sweetheart."

"It's okay." Will crawls to me, and I scoop him up. "He's all better now." I look at our son and he's staring at the phone, reaching for it. "Do you want to say hi to daddy?"

"Dada."

"Oh, my goodness. Did you hear him?"

"Yes. It's about time."

"Dada?" Will coos while trying to take the phone.

"Yes, it's daddy." He giggles when he hears daddy talking to him. Will gives my phone an open-mouthed, slobbery kiss, so I gently take it away and wipe it on my pants.

"Sorry, I don't know what you were saying to him, but he decided to paint my phone with his tongue."

"Oops. I said, 'give momma kisses for me.' You know what?"

"Hmm? What?"

"I can't wait to paint your pussy tonight with my tongue."

"Bastard. I'm so damn hard up." Luckily, I set Will on the floor again before angrily whispering into the phone. William's chuckle on the other end of the phone doesn't help. His throaty laugh goes straight to my clit. "I'm about to touch myself."

"If you do, I'm going to really spank your ass."

"Promises, promises." I hang up on him, tossing my phone on the sofa after I stand. "Jerk."

A year later

Scooping up Will, I carry him to the kitchen to feed him lunch. I need my own meal, but all I can think about is my husband's cock. What a terrible mom I'm becoming.

"Momma." He giggles, playing with his pieces of banana on his tray. "Bite."

"You eat your bites." I kiss his forehead and snack on some fruit. With one baby, our house is still pretty clean, so there's nothing for me to do except a load or two of laundry. I could take the baby out, but I know how William worries and doesn't want me out without a whole army of Steele Riders around me.

Will and I read a book together before I set him in his play yard to play without crawling while I start the laundry. Now that he's almost walking, it's a little dangerous to let him roam.

I hear the gate open, and I check out who's there, ready to grab my gun and take Will into the secure room William had built before Will was born. To my shock, it's my hubby. I gasp and open the door. He narrows his brows at me, storming into the house.

"What's wrong? You're home early." He's at least two hours early.

"You hung up on me. I don't appreciate that my dear wife. I'm going to have to punish you for that." He stalks toward me and closes the door behind him. I step back, banging my ass on the entrance table. "Trapped."

"Or maybe right where I want to be."

"Damn right, and I'm where I need to be. I love you, Mary." He thrusts one hand into my hair, cradling my skull while his other hand slides up my loose dress, pulling my panties to the side. William pushes two fingers into my soaking wet pussy.

"Oh my…I'm going to come."

"Good. I drove all this way to watch you fall apart for me. You know I don't like anyone to give you orgasms but me." He slams his mouth onto mine and pumps his fingers into me, hitting my g-spot. I pant and hold back my scream as I come. He drops to his knees and under my dress to lick up my release, making my orgasm last even longer. My head hits the wall while I grip his head and ride out the rest on his face. He drags me to the floor and frees his cock, slamming it into me as he lifts my hips. My back is off the ground while he sits on his heels, fucking me on a low angle, making sure to protect my belly. He leans forward and squeezes my tits, causing me to come again. He pulls out and stands, helping me to my knees and bringing his cock to my mouth. He's ready to explode. "Swallow." I suck him off, draining him dry.

That sets my pussy off again. I'm going to need another orgasm, and he knows it. He loves to prolong our loving as much as he can. He'll have his mouth on my cunt as soon as Will's asleep, and then I'll be getting a thorough fucking on our bed. I can't wait.

He adjusts himself after helping me to my feet. "Let me freshen up, and I'll take Will. You go get ready for an early night."

"What about dinner?"

"I'll cook and serve you in bed." He winks, walking away. I know damn well what he has in mind.

"I love you," I add. He stops, spins around, and

comes back to me, sliding his arm around my waist and kisses me thoroughly.

"I love you, my sweet felony." He walks away, and I can see his dick is hard. I'm one lucky woman.

THE END

About the Author

C.M. Steele is bestselling author on Amazon with over 100 books to read and enjoy!

C.M. Steele's Book List:

The Captive Series:
Luciano's Willing Captive
The Russian's Captive Sergei's Stubborn Captive
The Caught Series:
Caught In A Case
Caught Off Guard Caught in A Lie
Caught Crossing the Line
Caught Breaking the Law Caught Red Handed
The Kane Family:
His Christmas Rose
Her Christmas Surprise
His Candy Kane Christmas in July
The O'Connell Family:
Claiming Red
Burning for Claire
Claiming Abby
Reminding Red
Family & Friends:

Wanting it All
Lassoing His Cowgirl
Ben's Resolve
Chasing his Sunshine
The James Family:
No Choice
No Way Out
No More Waiting
Wolfe Creek Series:
Wolfe's Den
Beta: Her Alpha
Raging Kane
Written in History
Say Something Series:
Say Uncle
Say Please
The Cline Brothers of Colorado:
Whatever it Takes
Taking Whatever he Wants
Finding Paradise
Best Friends Series:
Always You
His Dirty Secret
Sleep Tight
The Middleton Hotels:
Built for Me
Built to Last
Built Strong
Built Over Time
Built Overnight

Southern Hospitality:
Down South
Gone South
A Steele Fairy Tale:
My Gold
My Forever
My Property
The Falling Series:
Falling for the Boss
Falling for the Enemy
The Lamian Wars:
Bound
Reveal
Release
All Hallows Eve
Keepsakes:
Keeping Blossom
Keep in Mind
Sweetheart's Treats:
Sweet Surprise
Doctor's Orders, Sweetheart
Sweet Surrender
Twin Sin:
Stalk Me Please
Sinful Intent
A Steele Riders MC Series:
Boomer
Mick
Jackson
Doc

Beast
A Rough Hands Novella:
My Miracle
Nailing my Wife
Obsessed Alpha Series:
Stone
Cole
Graham
Theo
Alessandro
Gimme Series:
Sugar
Luck
Rain
Cream
Heat
Others:
Conquering Alexandria
Taking the Bait
Loving My Neighbor
Mrs. Valentine
Scarred
My Christmas Gift
So Wrong
The Wedding Guest
Love Bites
Once Bitten
Christmas in Camden
Love Discovered
Unexpected

Rainy Days Stormy Nights
Sharp Curves